STRANGE VISITOR

Strange Visitor

LAURA CONWAY

Saturday Review Press
E. P. Dutton & Co., Inc.
1975

STRANGE VISITOR

I

Although the storm continued throughout the night, Clare Deering, who had thought it would be impossible to sleep, did in fact sleep soundly. But as a traveller at the end of a journey still retains an impression of jolting and swaying, so it seemed to her when she awoke to calmness and light that the pounding of the sea and the moaning of the wind was still in her ears.

She closed her eyes against the daylight, and would, had it been possible, have closed her mind against memory. Her first encounter with tragedy of such magnitude had left her with the conviction that life would never be the same again. She had seen the sleepy seaside village possessed as though by a demoniac force.

Even her own white painted home on the cliff had looked sinister and alien when, mounting the shallow cliff pathway, she had glanced up at it. It had been starkly outlined. Clutched by a livid hand, she had thought shudderingly, as forked lightning encircled it.

Clare shivered. It was a horrible picture which was etched before her eyes, though she had had no more than a glimpse of the night's tragedy, for Geoffrey had forcibly dragged her away from the throng of people clustering on the sands, had supported her up the cliff pathway, and when they were within the house, had thrust poor Cousin Phillis, babbling and terrified, into her arms. She, who as Cousin Becky said, should have set an example, was in far worse case than any of the hysterical servants.

It had been impossible for her to dislodge the clinging woman. Geoff said something about it being her business to look after them all at the house, and had attempted to go back, but he had stumbled on the downward path, severely wrenching his ankle, and a bare quarter of an hour later, had limped home.

She had had to minister to him as well as to Cousin Phillis and the other inmates of the house; tearing off his oilskins, his heavy boots and socks, and bathing and bandaging his swollen ankle.

The memory of this made her open her eyes wide, and she raised herself on her elbow to gaze at what could be seen of her husband in the wide feather bed. He usually slept with his face half-buried in the pillow and was doing so now. His thick, dark hair was rumpled, one arm flung out over the eiderdown. Clare looked at that thin, fine, tanned hand, and thought as she had thought many times before that it and its fellow were typically musician's hands; unusually long with more than the ordinary width between thumb and first finger; flexible wrists, a suggestion of nervous strength.

It was merciful, Clare thought, that Geoff's fall on the cliff had injured only his ankle, not one of the hands which created music; the music which was never quite good enough to satisfy him or the critics.

She slid quietly out of bed and went to the window to pull aside the curtain. Nothing she saw outside indicated that death and terror had been so near to them only six or seven hours before. The storm had died down as abruptly as it had arisen. The sun was shining, the trees were still; beyond the edge of the cliff the sea stretched blue and benign. But now Clare could not look at the sea without a shudder.

There was a light tap on the door and Joan came in with a tray. She said, 'I thought you mightn't be awake, ma'am, and that it would be a shame to disturb you, for most of the others are still sleeping, but then it seemed as though I'd better make sure . . . and as you *are* awake, you'll be glad of your tea, I dare say.'

'Yes, indeed,' Clare said, 'and I've slept later than usual. What sort of a night had you, Joan? How is Barbara?'

'Much better, ma'am. She was just saying she could fancy an egg for her breakfast. I'll get it for her before seeing to the other trays. She'll be up and about in another day or two, and then we shan't be at such sixes and sevens, and Cook

6

– who relies on her so – will be less grumpy. That's been tiring enough without the storm, and once I did get off, I slept like the dead.'

On the last word, the girl clapped her hand against her mouth, her eyes large and scared. 'Oh, what made me say that, when there must be so many who is – dead I mean? I got up just as the milkman came along, and he says there's hundreds have lost their lives . . . not a woman saved he says . . . nor a child.'

'Nobody can know for sure yet,' said Clare.

'Except there's been bodies washed up, and the lifeboat saved a few of the crew. The ship sank some miles off, nearer to Portmerron. It was blown right off its course . . .'

'It must have been, since it was making for Holyhead.' Clare poured out her tea, and drinking it, was grateful for the stimulating warmth.

Joan reached up to the hook on the door, and brought Clare her dressing-gown which had been hanging there, remarking that she'd catch her death of cold with next to nothing on.

'The sun's too warm,' Clare said. 'It's almost impossible to believe . . .'

'It seems as though we dreamed it all,' Joan agreed. 'It's to be hoped Mrs Marsh and that Adelaide get here on time as usual, for with Barbara laid up, we need them, and Nurse Martin's worn out sitting up with Mrs Redcliffe all through the night.'

'I did offer, but she refused,' Clare said.

'Well, it's she who's paid to look after her, not you.' Joan was often affectionately familiar. Clare did not resent it, scarcely noticed it. It was Geoffrey who sometimes objected, saying that Joan was inclined to take too much on herself.

But if she did it was natural enough. The household was in some ways madly eccentric. As for Joan, she had grown up with Clare, for Joan's widowed mother had been housekeeper to Clare's widowed father, and the two children had played together in out-of-school hours. Later, Joan had been employed as a children's nurse, and Clare had seen little of her. But when she and Geoffrey had married, Joan had

7

begged to be allowed to housekeep for them, pointing out that, as Clare intended to continue with the career which in the beginning had been the cause of so much opposition, and as her husband was a musician, she wouldn't have time to look after the house.

So it had been arranged, and Clare had never regretted the decision, for Joan was as adept at home-making as her mother before her. If necessary, she could turn her hand to anything, and as it was she valeted for Geoffrey, darned his socks, pressed his suits, and also looked after Clare's clothes. Hilary Moore, Clare's father, had married again, and was now living in France, and Clare was on friendly terms with Margery, her young stepmother, who envied Clare because Joan was so efficient and so devoted to her.

Sometimes Clare wondered if her marriage would have run as smoothly without Joan. She and Geoffrey were in love with one another; as much in love now, three years after marriage, as on their honeymoon. It sounded ideal, but Clare was frequently conscious of her inadequacy, and not only as a housekeeper.

For nearly two years they had lived in London, and then the death of Clare's famous uncle who had, against her mother's wishes and all the conventions which he scorned, encouraged her acting ability, and whose career had been an inspiration to her, had changed their lives. His bequest had not only brought them to Beechslope to the white house on the cliff called 'Welcomes', but had also entailed unusual responsibilities. Joan had coped with these.

Really they had put too much on her shoulders, thought Clare, with remorse. More than once just lately, it had struck her that Joan looked white and strained, and never more so than this morning. The storm, and the tragedy it had brought with it, might account for it, and yet Clare had the uneasy feeling that there was something more, and she said on an impulse of affection, 'When Barbara is about again, would you like to have a long holiday? If so, Mrs Moore would be delighted to have you for a time – she's not been too well, as you know.'

'Do you mean you want me to leave?'

8

The question was so unexpected that Clare stared. 'Good heavens, what put such an idea into your head?'

'Nothing . . . I only thought . . . if that was what you wanted . . .'

'Joan, how can you!'

There was an obstinate, withdrawn expression on Joan's face, her lips were set tightly together. She was a handsome girl, slenderly built, with regular features, and fair hair which she wore with a centre parting and coiled in a knot at the nape of her neck. Clare had never seen her looking anything but spotless, her plain dresses immaculate, her hair smooth, her movements deft and unhurried. She was two years older than Clare, who was now twenty-five.

'You know how often Mrs Moore has said she wished you had wanted to settle with her in France, instead of with me,' Clare reproachfully reminded her. 'It just struck me in a flash that you hadn't taken a holiday for ages, and that it would be a change for you.'

'I wouldn't live out of England for anything,' Joan said.

'I was only thinking of three or four weeks. But as you don't care for the idea we'll say no more about it.'

'Not unless you've got it in mind to be rid of me, ma'am.'

Not for the first time that scrupulous 'Ma'am' struck Clare as incongruous, though even in their childhood days Joan had always addressed her as 'Miss'. No doubt she had been instructed by her mother.

'Of course I haven't – I wouldn't know how to do without you . . . though I'd have to, if you were to get married. Don't glower at me like that, Joan . . . I was only trying to be unselfish. Oh dear, everything is frightful without starting off on the wrong foot first thing . . .'

At this pathetic plaint, Joan softened and said, 'You haven't . . . you gave me a turn, but I'm feeling all upset this morning, as though nothing will ever be ordinary again.'

'I know, I feel the same. It's as though the peace is spoiled. Last night the worst thing was to be so helpless – to know people were drowning within sight of land and safety; to know they couldn't be rescued – not a single life . . .'

'It wasn't to be, I suppose. But the sea was so rough,

9

most of them must have been too sea-sick to care whether they lived or died. I shall never forget the time I went on holiday to the Isle of Man, and was so ill I wouldn't have minded if I'd never got there.'

'Some of the passengers on that boat may have been good sailors,' said Clare.

Geoffrey turned over with a groan so protesting that Joan started and Clare glanced towards him. As he sat up, Joan made for the door, picking up *en route* a pair of trousers which hung over the back of a chair.

She said, 'These ought to have been taken away last night to dry, but I'll press them during the day, and they won't be any the worse. It's to be hoped Mr Deering's ankle is better and that he's none the worse for the drenching he got.'

'How long have you been awake?' Clare asked, as the door closed.

'Not long. I heard Joan rejecting the suggestion of a holiday with your father and Margery.'

'She thought I wanted to get rid of her permanently. Goodness knows why. I'd hate to do without her . . . though she's a queer girl in some ways. I've known her all my life, and yet I know next to nothing about her personally.'

'H'm. She's either reserved or dumb.'

'She's not dumb, she reads a lot. Perhaps she's a bit managing, but she's a marvel at her job, very domestic, and I'm fond of her.'

'Yes, you are, aren't you? Is that a cup of tea I see there?' Clare filled his cup and brought it to the bedside. He took it with his left hand, and with his right, drew her down to lean against his hunched knees.

'What a funny one you are,' he said. 'A biography of your handmaiden in a score of words. She's a dark horse. Is the milkman a beau of hers?'

'Not that I know of, Joan doesn't seem to take any interest in men. Do you really think she's deep?'

'I wouldn't know. Does it matter? My love, in spite of the exciting night we all had, you look as fresh as the dawn.'

'I can't believe it . . . and if I do, I must be very heartless.'

'Nonsense. Who would profit by it if you let your nerves run away with you?'

'Nobody, but I don't feel as placid as you say I look.'

'Not exactly placid; but as though nothing really gets under your skin. I'm not criticizing you. You're very much to my taste in that rose-coloured thing which ought to clash with your hair but doesn't. Is it new?'

'It's my old white negligee dyed. Joan did it – it had gone yellow with age.'

'The indispensable Joan again.'

'Sometimes I think you don't like her,' Clare said, puzzled, 'though you praise her and she looks after you so well – your clothes and everything. Geoff, do drink your tea while it's hot.'

She twisted herself out of his grasp, and his eyes followed her as she went to the window and looked out.

'Try to forget last night,' he suggested gently.

'As though I can – so soon. The milkman told Joan that not a single woman, not a single child, was saved.'

'That may be an exaggeration. Lord, though, how I wish I could have gone out in that boat.'

'I'm thankful you didn't. They had difficulty in getting back, and you'd have given up your place to another perhaps, and swum round on the chance of rescuing someone else.'

'I'm not that much of a hero.'

'You'd have taken a chance because you're a strong swimmer.'

'I doubt it – even a cross-Channel swimmer would have given up in such a sea. Where are you going?'

Clare, who had turned from the window, said : 'I'll have my bath, and then see to your foot. You'll have to rest it up today.'

'Not on your life. I'm going down to the shore after breakfast, but you can come with me if you like, and I'll lean heavily on your arm to prove that I didn't funk it last night.'

'As though anyone would think you did. Your ankle was dreadfully swollen and I expect it still is.'

'I'll have a look at it.'

Clare disappeared into the bathroom, but she was given barely time to run the water into the tub and slide down into it before Geoffrey appeared at the door.

'It's all right, I can stand on it,' he said, and then added with a grin : 'Don't look so cross; you didn't lock the door.'

'Because you hate it when I do.'

'You have such boiling hot baths, I'm always afraid you'll faint in them. Don't stay behind that steam barrier too long, or I shall come and pull you out.'

He smiled at her protesting gasp, and then went out, warning her that he would give her another five minutes and no longer. Clare, who knew that he would be as good as his word, did not dare to delay, though on this morning especially, it would have soothed her to soak in the water. The snag about marriage was that you no longer had any privacy. The hours you managed to steal for yourself were so few, and living at 'Welcomes' she had other claims upon her as well as Geoffrey's, which had always been demanding. She supposed she was an ungrateful woman for so many complained of being neglected whereas she would have welcomed a little neglect.

She dried her plump body, and was half dressed when Geoffrey called out to know if he could now run a bath for himself. She felt his hands on her bare shoulders.

'You little prude,' he said. 'How you hate me to see even an inch of you.'

'I don't; but there's a time and place for everything.'

'I only wish I could hit on it then.'

'You're ridiculous.' Clare shrugged off his caress and also the veiled reproach.

For a few minutes she had their bedroom to herself, and she luxuriated in it, as she sat before the looking-glass brushing her long, wavy red hair and listening dreamily to Geoff splashing, but there was the too frequent frown between her brows as she gazed at herself, wondering and regretting that nature had given her the type of good looks which, as Geoff sometimes said, were fraudulent. Red hair, long, greenish-grey eyes, a thick cream skin which did not tan, a mouth which was generously large and full, and a tall, voluptuously curved body. She hoped she would never get really fat, but thought this improbable, for she had not lost or gained a pound since she was seventeen. But how satisfactory it must be to look fair and cool and ethereal, and appeal to a man's intellect instead of his emotions.

Her type of good looks was a drawback to her. The stage parts for which she had been cast had rarely appealed to her. That, no doubt, was why she had had so few regrets on deciding to abandon her career.

When Geoffrey returned from his shower, she glanced at him more critically than was her custom, thinking that his looks also, with the exception of his hands, were at variance with his nature, for he was an idealistic, poetic person in many ways, yet had a stocky body, blunt features, a thick neck and powerful arms, and was a bare two inches taller than herself. He was so hirsute that it was necessary for him to shave twice a day, and his black hair grew in a low peak on his forehead.

It was queer, Clare thought, that they should have fallen in love with each other, for her ideal of masculine beauty followed her ideal of feminine beauty, and she had discovered it in the portraits of her Uncle Quentin, to whom this house had once belonged. He, in his time, had played Romeo and Bassanio and Orlando, as well as many a swashbuckling part in lesser plays. This had been before Clare was born, but as a romantic actor he had been greatly helped by his fine profile, and lofty brow. Clare had adored him. He had meant far more to her than her father.

Yet when she had met Geoffrey Deering she had been instantly drawn to him, though Quentin Moore had amusedly compared him with a good-looking Caliban.

Clare prided herself on having divined the essential fineness beneath his rugged exterior; his talent for composing delicate, haunted lyrics had given her a clue to his disposition.

'What are you brooding about?' Geoffrey asked.

'I don't know . . . the storm, us, Uncle Quentin . . . all a jumble.'

'You're an inveterate dreamer.'

'I haven't the time to dream now,' Clare said, rising. 'I ought to be helping Joan, who has her hands full with Barbara still laid up, and Cook in one long, continuous sulk.

'Joan takes it all in her stride,' Geoffrey said. 'Appetizing odours are arising from below. Breakfast is ready, I expect, and I'm ready for it. So should you be.'

'I can't make last night seem real.' Clare's expression was sad, remorseful.

'Just as well. That's one of your safeguards.'

'It's one of my worries.'

'Why?'

'Well, it's sort of dopey, and I wasn't always like this. I've a photographic kind of memory, as you know — that's why long parts rarely bothered me. I was an alert person until I married you . . .'

'Have I such a soporific influence?'

'I don't know . . . it's queer. It's as though I gave up a part of myself not only to you . . . But it's all a muddle — too confused to put into words.'

Geoffrey did not press for elucidation, though his small, bright, highly intelligent eyes were speculative as they rested on her. He merely said, 'Well, don't dawdle if you're coming with me down to the shore. I know you'll first insist on making the rounds to be certain all your interesting relatives have survived the perils of the night.'

*

Some ten years previously an extra wing had been added to 'Welcomes'. This was when, after a long tour of farewell performances, Quentin Moore had retired from the stage.

He had then intended to run a dramatic school and for a year or two had done so, but the venture had proved less popular and less interesting than he had expected, and the new wing, which comprised two large rooms of dormitory size, a small theatre and dressing-rooms and green room had fallen into disuse until a year before his death, when he had issued invitations for a family party at Christmas, and three of the guests who accepted his invitation for a week had stayed there ever since.

Quentin had been aware of the element of farce in the situation, but it was his misfortune to have a strong sense of family, and it was beyond his power to evict the two cousins and the half-brother who had all fallen on evil times and clutched at him pathetically.

Clare was never quite sure in what relationship Cousin Phillis and Cousin Becky stood to her; they were cousins at least three times removed; but Quentin's half-brother was also her father's half-brother, the son of their father's second marriage.

Hilary Moore, Clare's father, had shrugged his shoulders over Quentin's weakness, for he had no intention of acting as a lifebuoy to his impoverished relations, and when over a year ago, Clare had inherited 'Welcomes' and the bulk of Quentin's money, he had vigorously admonished her to rid herself of the three old people who had fastened themselves like barnacles on his brother.

Nothing was said about any of them in Quentin's will. Clare was his heir, with no conditions attached, and it was ridiculous, said Hilary Moore, to suppose that she could take such a burden upon herself. Theoretically, Clare agreed with him, but in practice she found it impossible to act with Spartan hardness. So also did Geoffrey, though he was fully alive to the absurdity of the situation.

There were several conferences, which had ended in their doing nothing whatever to rid themselves of the occupants of what was known as the theatre wing.

'It would haunt me if I made them leave,' Clare said unhappily. 'I never expected to have a lovely home and quite a lot of money, and I can afford to keep them – at least I can afford to keep Cousin Phillis and Uncle Noel. Cousin Becky pays all her own expenses except her actual houseroom.'

'And is more of a nuisance than either of the other two,' Geoffrey commented.

But he was also overwhelmed by the good fortune which had come their way; was even more in love with 'Welcomes' than was Clare, found it an ideal place in which to work, and was thankful that financial problems were no longer urgent ones, and that Clare's touring days were over for ever.

He agreed with her that it would be a scurvy act to throw three old people upon the world. Moreover, though he only touched lightly on this point, it was doubtful if any of them would consent to be dislodged. One and all of them declared that Quentin, expansively patriarchal, had said they were free to stay at 'Welcomes' indefinitely, and in order to evict them Clare would probably have had to go to law. This she would never do, and Geoffrey could not have found it in his heart to recommend such a course.

As a fact, he had an amused tolerance for the limpet-like trio, and it was the hilarious rather than the irritating aspect of the affair which impinged upon him.

All three were at one time stage favourites, and Cousin Becky had been outstandingly famous. Now she was approaching eighty, and partially crippled with arthritis, but she could never be forgotten. Again and again her name cropped up in theatrical memoirs; her birthdays were remembered and noted in *The Stage*, and similar journals, and occasionally some friend from the past, who had acted *ingenué* or *jeune premier* to her star rôle, would pay her a flying visit, just to see how the old darling was getting on.

Becky was not poor, but as she frankly admitted, she had loathed being cooped up in a London flat on her retirement, and when Quentin, remembering the long run some twenty years previously of a drama in which he had played her lover, with spectacular success, had asked her to spend that memorable Christmas week at 'Welcomes' she had arrived, complete with bath-chair and the pleasant middle-aged attendant whom she called Nurse Martin. But even so, the journey had tired the old actress, and her arthritis had been more than usually painful, and when bad weather set in, with snow and frost, it was obviously impossible for her to leave until conditions changed.

In due course they had, but by then Becky was a fixture, So was poor Phillis Gage, another remote cousin, who was some ten years younger than Becky, and who had been a charmer in her youth. She had had three or four husbands, occasionally the number varied, and she had a vague suspicion that there was a fifth whom she had forgotten) but they had either divorced her or been divorced, and with each successive husband, as she plaintively complained, there had been a mix-up in the financial arrangements they had made. They had each in turn stopped payment when she married again.

So dreadfully unfair, mourned Phillis, for they had also married, and she had never been the least spiteful or jealous about it. Her last husband she did remember clearly, for he had been years younger than herself, had deserted her, and had finally decamped to Australia with the last few hundred pounds she possessed.

In past days, Quentin Moore had had a sentimental tenderness for the vague and silly creature, and he had always kept in touch with her. After all, she was one of the famous theatrical Moore family, and they all stood by each other. In their way they were as famous as the Terrys or the Irvings.

When she caught a bad cold during that inauspicious Christmas visit, she was nursed back to health by Nurse Martin whose services Cousin Becky generously loaned. After which, weeks slipped by with Phillis enjoying a lengthy convalescence. She referred to herself as a visitor at 'Welcomes', and still talked of returning to the stage, if anything really worthy of her offered.

Quentin had given Phillis small sums, referred to as loans, and on his death he had left her a thousand pounds. Geoffrey and Clare suspected she had no other money whatsoever, but this sum, while she lived at 'Welcomes', could be eked out indefinitely. She possessed a large wardrobe of elegant clothes, and prosperous stage-friends sometimes sent her a scarcely worn dress or coat. Being deft with her needle, she could occupy herself happily enough in altering and renovating garments, and bringing them up to date. It was only very occasionally that she found it necessary to dip into her capital.

The third member of the community, Noel Moore, was also the youngest, and still in his sixties. He had been an excessively handsome young man, but his talent was mediocre. When a boy, he had devotedly followed Quentin's lead, who was in his fifteenth year when he was born. The older and brilliant brother was very attached to the younger one, though Hilary had always been contemptuous of him.

Certainly, when he was grown-up, Noel was a constant anxiety; more often out of a job than in one, and singularly lacking in ambition. But there were always women, usually older than himself, to adore him.

He had some slight taste for writing, and when he was in his late forties compiled a slender volume of fairy tales and poems, which somewhat surprisingly found a publisher. The sales were meagre, but the book attracted the attention of a wealthy American woman, whom Quentin knew slightly. She raved over Noel's poems, and on discovering that he was Quentin's brother, demanded an introduction to him. Ten years older than Noel, she nevertheless laid siege to him, and eventually Noel married her.

They had lived in America, and thereafter for some years all that was known of Noel was through his correspondence with his brother. His letters made it obvious that the marriage was a far from happy one, for although his wife was infatuated with him, Noel complained that he was a virtual prisoner, that she doled him out pocket-money at the rate of a few dollars a week, and was insanely jealous of him. Years later, when she died suddenly, she left her husband only a small income from a trust fund. Then Noel had written to Quentin to say that his one desire was to return to England. He was in poor health, and his sight was failing.

Quentin arranged for his passage home, and received him at 'Welcomes'. There, soon afterwards, Noel was operated on for cataract, an operation which was successful, but after years of idleness, he had no thought of returning to the stage. His small income would not have been sufficient for him to live in comfort, and he talked earnestly of writing another book. Quentin was regretting his retirement, had some thought of writing his autobiography, and Noel offered his help as amanuensis and collaborator. The work on the book was started, but only a few pages had been written at the time of Quentin's death, after which Noel announced that he intended to write his famous brother's biography.

This, to both Geoffrey and Clare, seemed a feasible project, and for months now Noel, in one of the large dormitory rooms in the theatre wing which he had adapted as a bed-sitting room, had been very important and preoccupied with what he described as intensive research work.

Quentin had bought him a typewriter, upon which he could be heard tapping away, and there was a growing pile on his desk, consisting of notebooks, photographs, playbills, and other research material.

*

This morning Clare found Phillis and Becky together in Becky's quarters, which was all to the good, for Geoffrey had given her a bare quarter of an hour for her round of visits, saying that if she were any longer, he would go off without her. It would save time to see the two cousins together.

Both Becky and Phillis considered this morning visit their due, and as Clare came in, Phillis said fretfully, 'How late you are! I'm surprised you could sleep at all. I've not closed my eyes all night.'

'Nonsense,' Becky said. 'I sent Marty to have a look at you before I dropped off myself, and you were snoring.'

'Gasping for breath, you mean. My asthma was torturing me.'

'That's a new one.' Becky laughed. 'Since when have you added asthma to your list of complaints?'

'I very rarely mention my complaints.'

Becky cast up her eyes to the ceiling. 'May you be forgiven for that, Phillis Gage.'

'You both look very bright and well,' Clare said, thinking it time to interpose.

'My bright and well look comes out of a box, dear,' Phillis said with a giggle. 'Becky may be above such aids, but I think that, whatever one's private sorrows, one should try to be attractive for the sake of others.'

This was a poisoned dart, for whereas Phillis, though still in a dressing-gown of coquettish pink satin and lace, had made up her face and could display a head of tight peroxided curls protected by a net cap, Becky, still in bed, looked brown and old and wrinkled. She was huddled in a heavy shawl, so often washed that it had faded to no particular colour, and her

19

grizzled hair was pinned on the top of her head in a scrawny bun. She had never been beautiful, but had had so much vitality and grace and talent, it had scarcely been necessary. Even now, when groomed and attired for visitors, she could look impressive, but on such an occasion as this, she strongly resembled a wizened monkey.

'Marty,' she now called in a voice still rich and resonant. 'Coffee for Mrs Deering.'

'No, really, Cousin Becky, I've just had breakfast,' Clare protested.

'Nonsense. Nobody refuses a cup of Turkish coffee, made as I've taught Marty to make it, the like of which you'd search for far and wide. My coffee is the sole reason why Phillis honours me with a visit at this hour.'

'I must say it's wonderful for pulling one together,' Phillis agreed, becoming more agreeable, 'but I'm always stimulated by your company, dear Becky. To anyone as nervous as myself, there's something so robust and reassuring about you.'

Becky snorted scornfully. 'You pamper yourself, girl. It would do you the world of good to get out for a brisk walk along the cliffs. I only wish I had the use of my legs, but after my massage Marty will wheel me out for a breath of fresh air. Why not come with us?'

'Oh darling, spare me.' Phillis shuddered prettily. 'It gives me vertigo to look down from such a height.'

'Phillis, to hear you, one would think your life had been a bed of roses before you came here. You'd be chipper enough and could still get a good stage part if you'd take yourself in hand, make up your mind not to be such a weak, self-indulgent fool, and when I say self-indulgent that's exactly what I mean . . .'

Clare saw the faded, artificial woman blench, saw her eyes widen in a scared expression as she muttered defensively, 'I don't understand you.'

'Oh yes, you do, and it'll be your ruination.'

Phillis's slight body sagged in the big chair, and Clare sighed with relief as Nurse Martin entered with the coffee tray. She mounted the short flight of steps to the enormous bed where Becky was enthroned and put it down on a table beside her.

'The biscuits from L'Abergies, Marty,' Becky ordered.

Phillis showed revived interest, for the biscuits, especially ordered from a Continental *pâtisserie* in London, were expensive and delicious, but Clare, as Marty approached her, insisted on only half a cup of coffee. The big room was oppressively warm and she was now longing to escape. Years ago, it had been the theatre which Quentin had had built for his school, but Becky who, on her arrival at 'Welcomes', had been given a good-sized dressing-room then furnished as a bedroom, had yard by yard and week by week encroached upon the adjoining theatre.

Luggage and furniture were brought in relays from London, and Quentin consented to remove the theatre seats. Eventually he had given his famous cousin a free hand. Thus the small stage had become her bedroom, the auditorium her sitting-room, and she had begged to be allowed to pay for the conversion of one dressing-room into a kitchen and another into a bedroom.

Conscious of the wealthy old woman's loneliness, Quentin agreed to this. He had pitied her profoundly, for Becky had been a queen in her own sphere, had fought with passion and courage against old age and the infirmity which was slowly crippling her, had refused the refuge of an expensive nursing home, and had shown — subtle flattery — that she set a high value on his companionship.

Now the long room was an expression of Becky's personality. Brocade curtains of a rich, deep red hung at the windows. Persian rugs covered the floor, and framed autographed photographs of theatrical personalities were hung on the walls; the furniture was massive and heterogeneous; some of it solid Victorian and mainly hideous; some of it Georgian. There were shelves overflowing with books; numerous small tables bearing lamps and ornaments and more photographs; chairs and sofas and cabinets. Her bed, gilt and ornate, and massed with silk cushions and padded silk quilts, had once belonged, or so it was said, to one of Charles the Second's many mistresses, and although Quentin was sure it was no more than a clever fake of a far later period, he had not disillusioned Becky.

A heavily carved screen stood before the glass swing-doors which had once divided the theatre from the foyer, and round this appeared a handsome head, with wavy grey hair, carefully arranged to cover partial baldness.

'Gallant as ever,' Noel Moore said. 'I feared I might find you both comatose after such a terrible night.'

'I'm too selfish to have found it terrible,' Becky said. 'All that forcibly struck me was that I was alive and in safety and, although nearly eighty, had with luck a few years to go, while unfortunate souls, many young enough to be my grandchildren, were perishing. It was a cause for jubilation.'

'My dear Becky, none of us believes you are as hard as that,' Noel said, coming farther into the room, and accepting a cup of coffee from Nurse Martin.

'Not hard, only human enough to congratulate myself on my good fortune. The old have to grab at what they can and hold on to it. We three have been very successful grabbers, as Clare at least must realize, though to do her justice I don't believe she grudges us our props and stays.'

'I don't,' Clare said sincerely.

Becky smiled at her, and in doing so a semblance of youth flashed back to her old face. 'Come here, my dear, and give me a kiss,' she said, and as Clare mounted the dais, the old cheek was laid against hers. 'Pretty creature you are,' Becky praised. 'You look like Demeter, which was a part I once played in a pretentious verse play which only ran for a week; you ought to have had a brace of babies by now. Goodness me, don't blush like that. It's only horse-sense, especially as you have given up acting, which is a very good thing, for you haven't the temperament, let alone the necessary talent.'

'Oh Becky, how unkind,' Phillis said reproachfully. 'When our beloved Quentin took us to see Clare at the Portmerron Theatre in that touring company, I for one thought she gave a charming performance as Portia.'

'What a night that was,' Noel remembered. 'My brother was so proud of you, Clare, and when we got home after

22

the long, cold drive, we drank your health in lashings of rum punch. Becky was benevolent enough then, I assure you.'

'I was tiddly,' Becky said with a chuckle, 'and Quentin was sure that Clare had inherited his gifts. By that time he had almost persuaded himself she was his daughter, not his niece – he always said her mother was the love of his life.'

'Everyone loved my mother from all I hear,' said Clare. 'I wish I could remember her better. She must have been beautiful, judging from her photographs.'

'Yes, in a milk and water way, but you're twice the girl she was.'

'I must go,' said Clare. 'Geoff is waiting for me. He wants to go down to the shore, and with his ankle swollen he'll find it difficult to manage the cliff pathway.'

'Let us hope,' Noel said, 'that the tragedy is less overwhelming than Joan reported it to be this morning.'

'She only repeated what the milkman told her,' said Phillis. 'They were chattering away at the side entrance in such loud voices that they woke me up. That's a very familiar young man, and I must say I'm slightly surprised at Joan, who has always struck me as being a most superior girl. He had his arm round her waist this morning.'

'Darned impertinent of the fellow,' Noel said.

'What a loss it would be to you, Clare, if she married,' Phillis said. 'You and Geoffrey depend on Joan for much of your extra comforts.'

'So does Noel,' Becky remarked. 'Joan never raises a finger for us, but she saves him a considerable amount in laundry, not to mention pressing clothes and shoe-polishing.'

'My dear Becky, you can take it from me that the girl is adequately recompensed for her services, and I imagine Clare has no objections.'

'None whatsoever,' Clare assured him hastily.

But Becky gave a salacious chuckle. 'Now what recompense would that be, I wonder? You're still a bit of a Don Juan, and according to Phillis, the girl is not as unapproachable as one might think.'

Clare was by this time threading her way through chairs and tables and footstools and bric-à-brac to the door. She lifted

23

her hand in a farewell which included them all and escaped. Nurse Martin followed her with a tray of used cups and saucers and the empty coffee-pot, and she said, 'Miss Redcliffe doesn't mean half she says, Mrs Deering. I know she sometimes sounds really spiteful, but her heart is in the right place.'

'Life must often be wearing for her,' said Clare understandingly, 'and although she never speaks of it, I know she suffers a lot of pain.'

Privately she wondered how Marty had endured such a job for so many years. She had been with Becky since the outset of her illness; had acted as an extra dresser to her, massaging her between acts, covering up her growing disablement to the best of her ability. When this had become impossible she had gone with Becky to spa upon spa, and when finally defeated, she had still stayed with her in the flat to which Becky had retreated and where she had been miserable and frustrated, which made it hard for all who came in contact with her.

Probably it was a relief to Marty when Becky settled down at 'Welcomes'. She had been more contented there; grateful to be in touch with Quentin, and free of boredom during his lifetime because of the many friends who frequently stayed with him; the stage people who were Becky's kind.

Nevertheless, it seemed a poor kind of life for Marty, who was still on the sunny side of forty. Everyone liked her; she was always kind, sympathetic, uncomplaining and cheerful, and possessed a comforting charm; partly due to a contented disposition and an excellent digestion.

'She's a good one at standing pain,' Marty said, 'and unselfish about that too. She keeps it to herself rather than have the others upset. With me now, when I'm massaging her, she bites her poor lips till they bleed rather than give a good groan, for it's a painful business to be pummelled and rubbed, though it's the thing that helps her to keep going.'

'You're very fond of her, aren't you?' Clare said gently, but also with some wonder, for although Becky was a stimulating person, she was not a lovable one.

'I'm grateful to her,' Marty said.

24

'I should have thought she was the one who ought to be grateful.'

'I wouldn't say that. I can do little enough for her; but she stood by me through a bad time, a very bad time it was, and I'm not one to forget.'

'I'm sure you're not.'

Marty went on as though musingly: 'And it's true, there's an affection – it's what gratitude brings with it, I dare say. If there's times when I get a bit tired, well then I say to myself, that when I most needed a friend, it was Miss Redcliffe who did all in her power for me; and that's why I wouldn't let her down or desert her however much I might want to.'

'But do you want to?' Clare asked, surprised.

'No, Mrs Deering, I've said I don't.'

But she hadn't said exactly that, thought Clare, puzzled and slightly uneasy. She had the impulse to ask further questions, but decided against it, realizing that Marty's expansive mood had already passed.

'Well, I must be getting on, there's plenty to do,' Marty said buoyantly. 'I hear Mrs Marsh clattering about on the stairs with her dustpan, and I'd better go and tell her what wants doing this morning. Don't you worry, Mrs Deering, because Barbara is still laid up. I can help with Mr Moore and Miss Gage until she's fit again. It's a tax on you, having to keep an eye on them in this wing, but as Miss Redcliffe says, your uncle must have wanted things to go on in the same way, or he'd have said otherwise in his will.'

'I'm sure of that,' Clare agreed.

'And Miss Redcliffe's generous. She knows you can't be expected to find the money for everything. She told me the other day that if Barbara had to have a long rest, she'd pay for more help than Mrs Marsh and Adelaide, and be glad to, not only for herself, but for the other two as well. In a way, it does her good to feel responsible, as though she's not yet laid aside and done for, which is what she dreads. She's made a home for herself, and she likes to feel she can help make a home for them too. She's got pity and understanding in her nature, as I should know.'

Clare murmured something non-committal, though she could not endorse Marty's tribute. Pity and understanding were not attributes which she would have connected with Becky Redcliffe.

2

'So the clan didn't keep you for an unreasonable length of time. I expected you to have difficulty in getting away, as they'd want to describe the harrowing effect the storm and the shipwreck had on them.'

'They were all in Cousin Becky's room; that shortened things,' Clare said, as she and Geoffrey started down the cliff pathway. He leaned on her arm, though not heavily.

'They'll none of them be bored today,' he said. 'They've enough to chew on for at least twenty-four hours, and each tragic detail will be well masticated.'

'They're not vultures,' Clare remonstrated. 'They're quite humanly distressed and shocked, even Becky, though she insists that if the other two were honest, they'd own that it's exhilarating to be still alive, when so many younger people, whose lives are more important to the world, are dead.'

'She would!' Geoff chuckled. 'She enjoys her rôle of ancient *enfant terrible.*'

'I sometimes think,' said Clare, 'it's because she can't bear to be ordinary. It pleases her to embarrass people, and she feels she has the right to say what she likes because she was a great actress.'

'What did she say to upset you this morning?'

'Oh, nothing much – I suppose most people would pass it off with a shrug and a laugh, and I wouldn't mind if we were alone, but when she says before others that I ought to have babies, that I have the proper physique for it, well . . . then I go red.'

26

'Officious old wretch,' Geoff said, satisfactorily annoyed.

'It didn't make it any better that what she said was true,' Clare murmured. 'If only you felt differently about children.'

Geoffrey pressed the arm upon which he leaned. 'I've explained my reasons, and you agreed with them. Now don't nag at me, darling, it's unlike you.'

'Does it have to be nagging when I try to make you understand that I have reasons too, and a point of view?'

'Try some other time,' he suggested, and winced as he trod on a loose stone which rolled away down the pathway.

'Did that hurt your foot?' Instantly Clare was all concern.

'Somewhat, though it's a very slight sprain – not much more than a wrenched tendon, I should think.'

'While we're in the village, we could get Dr Irris to look at it.'

'That's unnecessary. It'll be all right in a day or two. Tell me more of what happened this morning.'

'Nothing did – except the usual wrangling. Uncle Noel is the only sweet-tempered one, and even he was roused when Phillis criticized Joan. It seems she heard them talking this morning and looked out of the window, and she says the milkman was at the side door and had his arm round Joan. Both she and Uncle Noel agreed that that wasn't good enough for Joan, and then Cousin Becky had to chip in again and tease Uncle Noel by suggesting he made such good use of her, he'd hate to see her marry and leave. When he got annoyed and said he recompensed Joan for any services, she became Rabelaisian over the word "services", and accused him of still being a Don Juan.'

'Still? Was he ever?'

'Women were attracted to him when he was young, I think, and according to Uncle Quentin he married Isabel Cronert because she made him look a fool in public, wrenched some sort of proposal out of him, and then announced it to all her friends and had it put in the papers.'

'Poor old Noel – I can imagine it. He can be a pompous bore, but he's also a gentle soul.'

'He can be roused, though,' Clare said thoughtfully. 'He was furious this morning, and I escaped while the battle was at its height. That sort of thing is life for Becky, and Phillis enjoys it as a spectator, but I wish she would lay off him. I had a strange feeling this morning as though something was dreadfully wrong with us all – individually wrong, I mean. Life on the surface is so different from the life underneath.'

'That could be said of everyone, darling.'

'But Joan was especially odd this morning, and so was Marty. Uncle Noel and Cousin Phillis both seemed to be covering up something, and Becky was in a gloating kind of mood. Even when she spoke of Uncle Quentin, she gave his memory a glancing scratch. Something about my mother, saying that she was the love of his life, and then underrating her, too, describing her as a milk and water person.'

'I dare say she seemed so to that old tigress,' Geoff said reasonably, 'and she was always your Uncle Quentin's ideal, just as she was your father's. From all I've heard of her, she must have been a winning person.'

'Father couldn't bear to put anyone else in her place. When at last he did, I was glad, as you know, though I thought Margery might have a difficult time, even though Mother had been dead for so many years.'

'Do you think she has?'

'I can't be sure. She's a good correspondent and she writes long amusing letters, but they're rather impersonal as a rule. She did give me a glimmer, though, when she was expecting the baby, and that's why I was so dreadfully sorry it all came to nothing. She said if she had a son it would mean a lot, as that was something Father had never had; she said it would lay a ghost, and that from all she had heard of my mother, she was so sweet she wouldn't object to be laid away in lavender and only remembered occasionally.'

'Suggestive,' Geoff agreed. 'Did Margery know what she was taking on when she married?'

'To some extent, I suppose. Father talked a lot about Mother, he couldn't help it, and Margery insisted that if she married him, they must live in a different house. She knew it was all right by me, because I was on the verge of marrying you, and she'd heard Father say that when he retired he intended to live out of England.'

'They struck me as being happy enough when we saw them last year,' said Geoffrey.

'I think they are. Margery was wise to insist on Father retiring two years earlier than he need have done, for that gave them every excuse to live in France. Why not, as he had enough money? He must have realized that Margery's people didn't think it ideal for her to marry a man old enough to be her father; it was right for him to make a clean break. It seems to me that too many people are ruled by the past, tied by it – the old people in the theatre wing, and poor Marty as well.'

'Why Marty, of all people?'

Clare described their puzzling conversation, and ended by saying: 'I'm sure she's fond of Cousin Becky, but she evidently feels there's no choice for her. It's a hard life and a frustrating one for a youngish woman of so much energy, but in staying, she believes she's paying a debt, though what on earth can Becky have done for her worth the sacrifice of her whole life?'

'Nothing can be worth that,' Geoff said. 'People forge their own chains; probably Marty has – if she is in chains.'

'It seems a cruel waste, Geoff. She's a good nurse, but there's only routine work to do for Becky. Marty could be useful in the world, and if she had a chance, she might yet marry. Suppose Becky lives for several years and Marty's almost an old woman when she dies?

'I've little doubt Becky has provided for her in her will.'

'But if she wants her freedom, while she's still young enough to make something of it?'

'My dear girl, she's not forced to stay here, and although what she said was surprising, it may have been no more than a mood, and have meant little.'

Geoffrey had lost interest in the subject, and his manner was absent. They had completed their necessarily slow walk down to the shore, where many people had collected, and limping slightly but with added speed, Geoff moved towards them.

*

Clare listened, sickened, to vivid stories of the disaster. Only a few of the passengers and crew on the boat had been saved, and it appeared that the milkman had not exaggerated when saying that amongst these there was not a single woman or child.

There were bitter and scathing remarks, but Clare judged that nobody was really to blame. When it became evident that the ship was doomed, the women passengers, some with young children, had been put into the first two boats, but these when lowered had overturned. Later two other boats, after a severe battle, had reached the shore, and the occupants had been rushed off to the cottage hospital a few miles away; later still, a sprinkling of men, who by the aid of rafts and lifebelts had managed to keep afloat, were picked up by the lifeboat crew.

It was rumoured that there was some grave defect in the ship which had been launched a few months previously and had made but a few trips and always in good weather. Many of the rescued crew said that it was an unlucky ship. The captain had been lost, but this would have been his last passage; he had handed in his resignation because it was generally believed the ship was unseaworthy.

But such stories were to be expected after a tragedy, and there might be no substance in them.

At 'Welcomes', the usual morning paper was delivered, but Geoffrey bought a sheaf of others in the village. He was limping badly as they started to walk back by the sands. As 'Welcomes' was built on the cliff two miles from the village, they walked in solitude, but it was ominously littered with driftwood.

'I wish I'd been able to go out in the lifeboat,' Geoffrey said, moodily. 'They might have got nearer to the ship if they hadn't been undermanned. As it was, they had to turn back, though there was still room in the boat, for only really strong swimmers could be picked up.'

Clare thought and said that his aid was unlikely to have made the least difference. In that extraordinary and unnatural storm, the astonishing thing was that it had been possible to launch the lifeboat. Geoffrey was walking more easily now, and she was eager to be at home. Her gaze was

30

resolutely turned from the sea, which today she hated. It would have been less horrible had it been grey and dull, but there was a shameless treachery in the smiling blue which sparkled in the sunlight. It could have been a spring day instead of an autumn one. Those infantile waves, lightly tipped with white feathers, issued a tempting invitation. It was warm enough to swim, to take out a boat.

'I was told,' said Geoffrey, 'that that girl who married the Indian nabob was on board. The passenger list wasn't given in the papers this morning; too soon, I suppose, but the word was going around. As you knew her and were friendly with her, I thought it might be a bit of a shock to you.'

'Angela Rose?' Clare exclaimed.

'It's a fact, I'm afraid. One of the rescued crew – the purser – spoke of her. He was sure of her identity, though she had reverted to her single name, was no longer calling herself Maharanee.'

'Well, she had left him,' Clare said. 'We read about it in the papers. I suppose she might have been in Ireland – her people live there. She'd have gone back to them after the marriage collapsed.'

'According to the newspaper reports she'd been given a whacking sum of money. Not bad for a small-part actress. She was no more than that, was she?'

'Angela had only a small part when she was on tour with me, but she *could* act,' Clare said. 'She might have got to the top.'

'Did you like her?'

'Yes, I did, though she wasn't popular. For some reason or other she got the name of being a Jonah, and that's awful if you're on the stage. When we started to do bad business soon after Angela joined, people said it was only to be expected.'

'Did she know she'd been tagged in that way?'

'Perhaps. We didn't talk about it. She was an odd girl. Her mother was a Spaniard and her father was a Scot; but she told me once that she had "the sight", and could sometimes foretell the future. I begged and implored her not to tell me mine, it was too scaring, and she laughed and said she wouldn't. Oh Geoff, it's terrible to think she's dead. She was younger than I – she can't have been more than twenty-four, and so full of life; a mischievous, defiant kind of life. When I heard she was marrying an Indian prince, it seemed just like her – she'd be so tempted by all he could give her. She'd have risked it.'

'A good many girls would have risked it, knowing that whatever happened they'd get a fortune settled on them,' observed Geoffrey.

By this time they were climbing the cliff pathway, but Geoffrey's foot appeared to be giving him little trouble. They arrived at the top, and now 'Welcomes' was only a few yards away, and they were immediately sighted by Joan, who came swiftly along the cliff to meet them.

'You'll have done your foot no good by that climb, sir,' she said. 'When I heard you'd gone down to the village I knew it would be too much for you. I saw your flask of brandy on your dressing-table, and I brought it along with me.'

'Thoughtful of you,' Geoffrey acknowledged, and when Joan offered him her arm to lean on, he accepted it.

'You told me your ankle wasn't hurting you,' Clare said, feeling guilty, and fleetingly wondered why she found it necessary to justify herself to Joan.

Geoffrey had swallowed some of the brandy, and now had peered into the narrow neck of the bottle and said : 'Hallo! That's the last drop, though I refilled it last night.'

'I'd got the flask in my hand, meaning to come down to meet you when Nurse Martin took it from me,' Joan said. 'There's been a lot happened since you went off this morning. A passenger who was on the ship was brought here, and Nurse grabbed the flask. She must have spilled half of the brandy, for it wasn't possible to get more than a few drops into the poor thing's mouth.'

Both Geoffrey and Clare stopped short to stare at her, and Geoffrey said, 'Alive?'

'Oh Geoff, of course – if they wanted brandy,' Clare said excitedly.

'It seems scarcely possible after all these hours in such a storm, and why 'Welcomes,' for heaven's sake? It's right out of the way.'

'Better to let Miss Redcliffe tell you,' said Joan. 'She vowed she'd have my life if I did. She's got her chair under the veranda, determined to be the first to see you. Such excitement! Miss Gage and Mr Moore have been running round in circles. The doctor has been, and says he hopes she will be all right, and the gentleman who carried her in has gone off, though Miss Redcliffe did her best to keep him. He said he'd be back this evening to find out how things were.'

'Carried *her* in.' Clare repeated the three words which conveyed most to her. 'Then it's a woman.'

'Yes, ma'am; a young woman too, from what I heard. I didn't catch a sight of her myself.'

'Oh Joan, how wonderful!' Clare's eyes were misty with tears.

Leaving Geoffrey to make his slower progress on Joan's arm, she ran swiftly to the house, to be intercepted by Becky, who propelled her wheel-chair down the garden path to meet her. 'If Joan told you . . .' the old woman began threateningly.

'She didn't. You tell me yourself.'

'It will be a shock to you, but a welcome one, I'm sure,' Becky said. 'The poor girl, or perhaps I should say the fortunate girl, for she's likely to pull through, is someone you know. She was conscious for a few minutes and was able to tell us who she was, and then, battered about though she is, I recognized her from the newspaper pictures . . .'

'I know what you are going to say. It's Angela Rose,' exclaimed Clare.

*

As a general rule, Becky preferred to lunch in her own rooms with Marty, but today there was so much excitement that they all gathered together at the long table in the dining-room.

'Welcomes' in itself was quite a small house, which accounted for the fact that Quentin Moore had lodged his three relatives in the theatre wing, where there was space to spare for them.

In 'Welcomes' proper, there were a living-room, a dining-room, and a room which had been called the garden room, now used exclusively by Geoffrey. Here he had his piano and composed his music. Above, there were four bedrooms, one large and with a bathroom of its own; the other three were small guest rooms, with a communal bathroom. The maids had their quarters over the coach house.

In Quentin Moore's day the guest rooms had been occupied nearly every week-end, but this was rarely so now that Clare was the owner of 'Welcomes'. She had fewer friends, found less pleasure in keeping open house, and Geoffrey, when he was working, had no time to spend on entertaining visitors.

Sometimes Clare thought she would have been lonely had it not been for the occupants of the theatre wing who one way and another kept her busy, and made constant though trivial demands on her. Joan was an expert housekeeper, the cook had been in Quentin Moore's service since she was a young woman, Barbara in her way was as capable as Joan, and there were two daily helps. There was little enough for Clare to do, and sometimes she thought regretfully of her stage career, and wondered if it might not be better to start again. But if she did, it would mean leaving Geoffrey here, for he, certainly, had no inclination to return to London.

Moreover, though she would probably have little trouble in getting parts, these were unlikely to be important ones. It would be ridiculous, now that there was no financial necessity, to work so hard at a profession which now meant little to her. She thought vaguely that she ought to take up tennis or riding, but she had no enthusiasm for either; nor was she particularly addicted to the tea-parties which were given by her local acquaintances.

Yet sometimes it was dreary to live so much amongst the old, listening to Becky's reminiscences, advising Phillis about her clothes, attentive when Noel mapped out a plan of the biography and showed her the exercise books he had already filled with closely scribbled notes. Geoffrey, during his long hours of work, was no companion to her: it distracted him to have her in the same room though she might be quiet and almost motionless.

34

Today, as Clare looked round the lunch table, she visioned a very different scene; not old people, but children should be there for the midday meal – her children and Geoffrey's. The familiar resentment swelled within her. It wasn't right or fair now that they were in the fourth year of their marriage.

'Dear Clare,' Phillis said, breaking in upon her mood, 'how wonderful to think it is your friend who has been saved from death. Did you know she was on that ill-fated ship?'

'Only a few minutes before I heard she had been brought up here.'

'What a dreadful shock for you.'

'I hadn't had time to realize it, and although I liked Angela, we weren't close friends, and I had lost touch with her. I haven't toured since I married, and Angela never played in London.'

'She had phenomenal luck to meet a fabulously wealthy Indian prince when she was in the provinces,' Becky said. 'Where has she been living since the divorce? Where did she live during her marriage?'

'Not in India. The Maharajah was deposed some years ago. I think he had a house in the South of France.'

'Deposed or not,' said Noel, 'he must have been wealthy, and it was said at the time of the marriage he had settled a fortune on her. She must be one of the lucky ones.'

'Yes. Perhaps she is lucky – to herself,' Clare said.

Becky looked at her sharply. 'Why do you say that?'

'I was only thinking she couldn't have made the Maharajah happy.'

'You've not yet told us, Cousin Becky, why she was brought here,' Geoffrey said. 'Start on the story while I carve the ham – it seems to be generally agreed that it's your story.'

'So it is, for I was the first to see her,' Becky pronounced regally. 'Or rather I saw *him*. Marty and I were out on the cliff, and then I saw him toiling up the cliff, and it might have been a life-size doll he'd got, thrown over his shoulder. I realized it was someone from the wreck, though I was sure it was a dead body. He was making for the house. I didn't want him to take it there, and I shouted out to him, and then of course Marty, who'd had her back turned, saw him too, and I made her wheel my chair, and we were just at the top of the path when he came level with us – and really, my dears, he was quite the most handsome young man I've ever seen – though I've seen some in my day. Golden hair, if you can believe me, and perfect features and a skin as fine as a woman's but not a sissy – far from it. Muscles like steel he must have, to carry a girl's dead weight up the steep pathway. He knew what was in my mind before I could get the words out, and he said : "Don't be frightened; she's alive. I found her lying on the shore farther along. She was on a raft, and it washed her up on the rocks. I'll lay her down here on the grass, while I go up to the house and see if someone can get in touch with the hospital." But of course when I heard the girl wasn't dead I told him to carry her right in. I couldn't do anything else.'

'Of course you couldn't,' Clare agreed.

'Joan,' said Marty, 'was crossing the hall with your brandy flask, Mr Deering, and I just wrenched it out of her hand.'

'Marty!' thundered Becky.

Marty giggled excitedly. 'I'm sorry, Miss Redcliffe, you go on then . . .'

'You can give me time to draw my breath, I suppose.'

Geoffrey handed two plates of ham to Joan who was waiting, and brought two more plates himself, to put before Phillis and Noel.

'Hurry up, Cousin Becky,' he said. 'What did this Hercules or Adonis do next?'

'Put her down on the fur rug in the hall, and you'd better have it dried for she was dripping water all round her. He managed to make her swallow some brandy, and Marty sent a message to the doctor, and I got a good peek at her and was just thinking there was something familiar about her face, bruised and white though it was, when she opened her eyes and looked at her rescuer.'

'Poor girl, how terribly grateful she must have been to him,' Phillis breathed romantically.

'Well, so you'd expect, but I dare say she was too far gone to be grateful, or even to see him distinctly, for she just rolled over on the rug, and hid her face and was shaking all

36

over, but Marty knelt down and petted her a bit, and then asked her her name, and she said with teeth chattering that she was Angela Rose. We didn't get another word out of her, for she fainted dead away, and I took it upon myself to see that she must be put to bed with hot-water bottles in the blue room, and Marty and the young man carried her up there. He left her with Marty, and when he came down he looked so white and drawn that I told him he needed a spot of brandy as much as Angela Rose had needed it. Joan had made off with the flask, saying she was going to meet you, Geoffrey, so I asked him to wheel my chair into the theatre wing and to find the bottle I always keep handy for emergencies, and we talked while we waited for Marty. He didn't stay more than ten minutes or so, but said he'd call back this evening.'

'But who is he? Where does he live?'

'Naturally I asked him that myself, and he said at Walnut Tree Cottage.'

'Good lord!' exclaimed Geoffrey.

'Exactly. I must have looked a bit goggle-eyed, for he asked me why, and although I hedged, he got it out of me, but he didn't turn a hair.'

'It's odd that nobody else had told him,' Clare said.

'There hasn't been much time. He only took the cottage about a fortnight ago—furnished, of course, though he says he's put in bits and pieces of his own. It seems he's an artist with a taste for painting sensational kind of pictures. He was at Carvina at the time of the earthquake last month, and although it must have been dangerous, he painted a picture with the volcano erupting before he got away. Then he had a fancy to do some seascapes, and saw an advertisement for Walnut Tree Cottage which was to let furnished, and he has taken it for a few months. Naturally the agent didn't put him off by telling him its history, though it's doubtful if he'd have cared. It would take something to frighten that young man.'

'One mightn't be frightened—exactly,' Clare said, 'but at the same time one wouldn't want to live in a place which was associated with so much horror. Is he alone there?'

'No. He says he has his man with him; an old family servant, I gather. It was evident while he talked that he is a young man of birth and fortune, possibly a bit of a genius as well. A really interesting young man, which so few good-looking ones are.'

Geoffrey said with a laugh, 'He certainly won your heart, which isn't too easy.'

Becky chuckled. 'My dear Geoff, I'm as vulnerable as most vain old women. Believe it or not, that boy — he can't be much more : in his late twenties, I imagine — knew of every important part I'd ever played. He had seen me in a few, years ago, though he must have been a child then, but more intelligent praise I've never heard. There's no denying it warmed my heart.'

Geoffrey smiled at her kindly. 'I dare say it did, but there's nothing so extraordinary about it. There's scarcely a book of theatrical memoirs which doesn't give a chapter or so to you.'

Becky glowed at the tribute, and generous in her turn, said that she had mentioned Geoffrey's music to the appreciative stranger, who was well acquainted with certain of his songs, and greatly admired some of them.

'That's more than I do,' Geoffrey said with a wry smile. 'I'd just as soon most of what I've composed was forgotten.'

'Geoff, you've given pleasure to so many,' Clare said, 'and your best work is yet to come. This Mr — er — but what is his name? Did he tell you, Cousin Becky?'

'He did. It's an odd one. Nairn.'

'You must have had an interesting talk,' Phillis said enviously. 'If he's such a keen theatre-goer, he may remember my performances as well as yours. After all, they are more recent.'

Becky shrugged her shoulders and said this was more than likely, though for her part she wouldn't care to be remembered by the stupid drawing-room plays in which Phillis had chiefly shone.

As the two old ladies glared at each other, Clare broke in to say : 'All this is very interesting, but it's not so important as Angela. What was the doctor's report? All I've heard

38

so far is that he gave her a sedative, and said that if she wakes, she's to have light food such as beef-tea or egg-nog.'

'Marty can tell you about that,' Becky said and Marty obeyed.

'Dr Irris hopes there's nothing seriously wrong. The poor girl has been knocked about, of course; she has some nasty bruises, and she is suffering from shock and exposure, but there are no dangerous injuries, and if she escapes pneumonia, she ought to come through all right. Dr Irris says he'll be round again this evening to see her.'

'It's a near miracle,' Geoffrey said.

'It nearly always is miraculous when people escape injuries in such disasters, but it frequently happens,' observed Noel. 'Was the girl lashed to the raft?'

But nobody had any idea, and Becky said impatiently that it scarcely seemed to matter; the important thing was that she was alive, and that in all probability a little careful nursing would soon see her perfectly fit.

When the meal was over, Clare went upstairs and softly opened the door of the blue bedroom. It was small but attractively furnished in blue and white. The view from the window was of the orchard and the fields beyond, which was just as well, Clare thought. Nobody who had survived a shipwreck would find any immediate pleasure in gazing at the sea.

Angela Rose was a small, slight girl, and she was lying very still in the narrow bed. Dark, elfin locks were brushed back from her face, and cuts on her forehead and on one cheek had been dressed by Dr Irris. The plaster strapping, and the fact that she had been put into one of Marty's night-dresses which was far too big for her, made her look additionally pathetic. The robe was high-necked and long-sleeved, warm and comfortable and made of some woven material. The cuffs of the sleeves fell over Angela's hands, which rested on the coverlet, and half concealed them. Her eyes were closed, but although she lay so silently, her expression was not peaceful. Her brows were drawn together frowningly, and her mouth compressed as though in pain.

Drugged and sleeping heavily, it was probable that she was still dreaming of the horrible experience she had undergone.

Her hand moved convulsively and Clare put her own hand over it, trying wordlessly to convey reassurance.

There was a ring on the third finger of Angela's hand, and feeling it beneath hers, Clare involuntarily looked down at it. Two rings actually, but the wedding ring was almost entirely covered by a huge emerald set in diamonds. A fabulous ring, thought Clare, no doubt the gift of Angela's ex-husband.

Clare had liked Angela, but she had always thought her strange; so had many other people, and Angela had known this and had been amused by it. She had played up the vague suggestion of mystery, but not to Clare. Though she had boasted of having 'the sight', she had not enlarged upon this gift when Clare said that to her it was a terrifying one. She realized now that it must have given Angela a sense of power to inspire fear, even if such fear were mingled with aversion.

Clare removed her hand, and was about to depart when the girl's heavy lids lifted and stared up at her. They were remarkable eyes, set in a small, pointed face. Deep-set, large, and of a piercing shade of blue, they were shaded by very dark lashes and heavy white lids.

'Angela – it's all right; you're safe now,' said Clare.

'Are you dead too?'

The words were uttered in a thread of a whisper, and before Clare could reply, another sentence formed and was murmured exhaustedly: 'I didn't think – why are we together? Now you . . .'

'Neither of us is dead,' Clare said. 'You were rescued, and this is my home. You were brought here.'

'By – by . . . *he* brought me?'

'Yes. And he's coming back this evening to find out how you are. My old Cousin Becky says you saw him for a moment when you were conscious.'

'Yes – I saw him.'

'He helped to save your life. Cousin Becky says he's a most beautiful young man.'

Angela murmured something incoherent, then she shuddered and once more closed her eyes.

3

Nichol Nairn walked along the sands with the easy springing gait which Clare had first thought unusual but which
she had soon come to associate with him. It occurred to her
that he probably associated her with a garden, for he generally arrived at 'Welcomes' around noon, an hour which on
fine days Clare kept for gardening. Mostyn, the regular gar-
dener, was afflicted with rheumatism, and although the half-
grown-up son of one of the fishermen came along for some
hours each week to do the hardest work, it was Clare who
weeded and mowed the grass, who pored over seed catalogues
and had built a rockery.

It was pleasant work, but apt to engender backache : therefore from time to time she rose to flex her arms and legs and
stretch her back. It was while she was doing this that she
had looked down upon the sands and seen Nichol Nairn
making his easy way up to her.

She waved and he waved back. From the garden room came
the sound of Geoffrey's music. He was working on a new
composition, really working, thought Clare, not gliding from
one tuneful phrase to another. This thing which his mind
laboured to evolve must be more difficult, more ambitious,
and there was little melody in it as yet. A rumble of chords,
a dissonant clatter of treble notes, and a plaintive bar repeated
more than once.

'Storm music,' said Nichol Nairn behind her.

She started and looked up. 'How quickly you got here, and
how silently. I didn't hear a sound.'

'Crêpe soles,' he said, indicating his sandalled feet.

'Just let me plant these few bulbs, and then I'll give you
a sherry,' Clare said. 'Oh, drat gloves,' as one of the thick,
shapeless ones she wore fell into the trench. 'I wouldn't wear

41

them, only Geoff makes such a fuss if I don't. I like the fee
of the earth, but he says gardening makes the hands horrible
– hard and seamy.'

'Demeter wearing gardening gloves seems scarcely in character,' Nichol said.

'Queer you should call me that. Cousin Becky does occasionally.'

'She's a perceptive old lady but it occurred to me the
first time I saw you.'

Clare shrugged and moved towards the house. The stum-
bling music suddenly resolved into a cannonade of chords. She
stood for a moment to listen and then said : 'I dare say it is
storm music. Geoff still has it ringing in his ears. There was
a terrible, fierce kind of music in it, or there could have been
to a person who makes music. But it's quite different from
his usual sort of thing.'

'You are a musician yourself?' Nichol enquired.

'No – or only in a very mediocre way. I can warble the
popular songs, and read music if it's not too difficult. I certainly couldn't compose.'

'Your husband has had some very charming songs and
studies published; they're popular.'

'I wish that satisfied him. I get a kick when I hear a
restaurant orchestra play them, or on a London barrel organ,
but Geoff doesn't. He deplores what he calls his facility.
He likes making money of course, but he says he's spoilt for
better work.'

'It's always the same,' Nichol said. 'The popular writer of
romances, the artist who turns out flower paintings and is in
demand as an illustrator, the actor or actress who has made
a name by polished acting in competent comedies, all hanker
for the plaudits of newspaper critics, which would probably
not advance them in the slightest.'

'Surely it's very understandable,' Clare said, pouring him
a glass of sherry but contenting herself with a table water.
'People who create want intelligent appreciation, they want
the notice not only of the library reader who will demand
a romance or a thriller not caring who has written it, but
of those who think and are capable of criticism. The financial

reward is pleasant, but not enough. Besides, most creative people want to be remembered for all time, not only to give present pleasure.'

'Very greedy of them,' said Nichol, laughing, 'but I doubt if you're right. If you are, the Chamber of Horrors at Madame Tussaud's would be an incentive to murderers.'

'That's an extreme illustration.'

'Yet, for all we know the shades of those who have suffered judicial murder may visit a place where they can still see themselves as they were in real life.'

'What a horrid idea!'

'Perhaps if there is a general longing to be recognized by posterity, it's because men and women are fools enough to believe that is their only immortality.'

'Which would be dreadful if it were true.'

'Dreadful to face oblivion?' Nichol asked.

'I think so. Don't you?'

'I can visualize worse things.'

Clare shivered, though she could not have told why. 'Would you be content for your pictures to be seen and praised only by your contemporaries?' she asked.

'So far as I know they will never be seen by anyone else; and it would not concern me if they were seen by nobody but myself.'

'You don't worry about the money angle then?'

'I've no need to. I'm what you would describe as rich, though money means little to me. I prefer to live simply. It's true I like to travel. People interest me, but it's easier to get to know them intimately if you are not set apart by the barrier of luxury.'

'Sometimes you speak in such an odd way for a young man.'

'How old are you, Demeter?'

'It's ridiculous to compare me with Ceres.' Clare laughed. 'If it's a commentary on my buxom appearance, there are many women who are plumper. As for age, I'm twenty-five, and you can't be much older.'

'If I wanted to be mystical,' Nichol said, laughing also, 'I should say that I am not – in this incarnation. Demeter, or Ceres, if you prefer her more common name, is immortal,

43

and so were all the gods and goddesses and the dryads and nymphs of those days.'

'I'd hate to think I was the reincarnation of anyone, even a goddess,' Clare said. 'It's much more satisfactory to be sure that one's individual self is straight from the mint. But you certainly do succeed in making people feel curious about you. You seem candid and ordinary, and yet you're mysterious. For instance, you speak English without an accent, but your name doesn't sound English, and your looks aren't, either. We've talked a lot together this week, but you've told me really nothing about yourself.'

'Are you curious? That surprises me. It isn't in character.'

Clare gazed at him as he sat leaning back in a comfortable chair, lazily twirling the stem of his glass, idly contemplating the wine which he had barely tasted.

'I'm not exactly curious – but interested,' she explained. He was, as Becky had said, extremely good-looking in a rather unusual way. He was clean-shaven, had thick, wavy, golden hair, eyes which were black, or looked black, for they might be no more than a very dark grey, fine chiselled features and an unusually fair skin. He was not very tall and was slenderly built, but nevertheless there was an elusive suggestion of strength in his spare body.

'I'm quite willing to gratify your – interest,' he said with a smile. 'I'm of mixed parentage . . . very mixed. My father was part Russian, part Greek, born in England; my mother was a mixture of Irish and Dane, with a dash of Italian. Both died years ago. I was educated in England, had a smattering of various talents, but there was no necessity to earn my daily bread so I've drifted through the years with no settled home and no definite occupation. I've travelled a good deal, and it was when I was in France last year that I met Angela. She wasn't too happy, was on the verge of parting from her husband, and we became friendly.'

Clare was considerably startled. She said, 'I'd no idea she'd met you before the other day.'

'Really! I thought she would have told you so.'

'She's been too ill to talk much. As you know, Dr Irris was afraid she might develop pneumonia, but she didn't,

44

and she'll be able to get up tomorrow. Of course I gave her your note and your flowers – wonderful-looking flowers they were too : I've never seen anything like them. Some kind of orchids, aren't they?'

'Yes – rather rare. I was in London the other day and saw them in a shop and I hoped they would appeal to Angela. She likes orchids.'

Clare did not say that Angela hadn't liked his orchids, which were of a dark purple shade and splashed with orange. She had gazed at them with aversion and had asked Clare to give them to someone else. Eventually they had been bestowed on Phillis, who had put her head round the door to enquire how Angela was, and had gone away with the air of a leading lady clasping a bouquet at the fall of the curtain.

'She will see me tomorrow, no doubt,' Nichol said. 'She must realize I've been very concerned about her.'

'I told her.' There was a puzzled uncertainty in Clare's eyes as they rested on him. 'It's an amazing coincidence that you found her, should have known her, should have been her friend.'

'A coincidence, yes,' he agreed. 'But I wouldn't call it amazing. I've met quantities of people. One does, if one travels for years on end. Most of us, if we can afford it, occasionally visit the Riviera or Italy or Switzerland. Angela lived for eighteen months with her husband near Cannes in a gorgeous monstrosity of a villa, and there was scarcely a personable visitor to Cannes, and many who weren't personable, who didn't get invited sooner or later to one of the dances or parties given there. It so happened that Angela and I had interests in common, and we met more than once.'

'What I meant was, that it's a coincidence you should have been staying here at the time she was on that boat. This isn't a place which many visit. We haven't a tourist season or a proper hotel – only an inn.'

Nichol shrugged and said, 'Odder things must have happened to all of us. A quiet place is ideal for my purpose, and it's surprising that artists have not found it out and settled here.'

'They'd have to build, or to live in tents if they wanted to settle. Few people let their houses, and there aren't many people except the fishing folk . . . just the two doctors, and the vicar and a few retired couples. Walnut Tree Cottage wouldn't have stood vacant, it would have been bought up by somebody, save for the story attached to it. Cousin Becky told you about that, so she said, and I rather wonder . . .'

'That it didn't give me a distaste for the place? Why should it? It's an old cottage – part of it early Tudor – and all old houses have their histories. No doubt many of them are sinister.'

'But what happened to Walnut Tree Cottage was recent, not in Tudor times. The villagers shun the place.'

Nichol laughed. 'Don't I know it? My man, Links, tells me that the milkman bolts after he has delivered the milk, and that none of the other tradesmen are keen on delivering things. He tried to find a woman to come in to clean each day, but he gave up. Not one would consider it.'

'They think it's haunted or cursed.' Clare's voice was troubled.

'My dear girl, the tragedies which happened there were due to the characters of the people concerned, not to the house. A man and a woman married, didn't get on, quarrelled, drank too much, ran into debt. The woman was found at the bottom of the stairs with her neck broken; the man was suspected of murdering her. He stood his trial and was acquitted and came back to the cottage. There he was shunned because people believed him guilty. A few weeks later, he too was found at the bottom of the stairs, also with his neck broken – either suicide or accident – probably the former. A miserable story, but why should it affect the house?'

'It seems to me likely that any place in which such an awful thing happened would be affected,' Clare said. 'The memory of it would linger there for ever.'

'That's a ridiculous theory. If it were any more than a theory, half the world would be haunted; but houses and even towns have been built upon ground where bloody battles were fought and thousands of men died in agony.'

'You haven't heard all the story,' said Clare.

'Have spectral figures been seen wandering around and

46

wringing their hands?' Nichol asked mockingly.

'Not as far as I know, but according to the evidence, that man's death wasn't a clear suicide or accident. When he was found, there were bruises on him, not caused through the fall. There were the marks of fingers on his neck, and there were signs of — of a struggle. The furniture in his room was thrown about, the carpet in the passage was rucked up, there were scratches on the banisters, as though he had clawed at them, trying to save himself . . .'

'You think he was murdered, too? By a burglar perhaps?'

'Nothing was taken from the house, and it's not what I think, but what others think. They believe it was she who came back and killed him as he killed her. The judge and jury let him off, but she wouldn't. It was glossed over at the inquest . . . it was suggested the man had a fit, and had caught at his own throat, staggered around in a paroxysm . . .'

'But that's a perfectly plausible explanation,' Nichol said. And then as Clare was silent : 'It doesn't seem plausible to you?'

'I don't know. It was a ghastly thing to happen, and I wish you weren't living there. We none of us like to think of you living there.'

'How quick you are to impress on me that it's not your personal anxiety.'

Once or twice since she had become friendly with Nichol, Clare had experienced unease, as though she were being drawn into an alien world, or was on the verge of becoming involved in something to which she could not put a name. A tangle, a drama, a tragedy — no word fitted the premonition, but now at the petulant note in Nichol's voice, she was suddenly at her ease.

'I should be anxious and disturbed about anyone who rented that horrible cottage.'

'I'm aware of that. Well, it's something that you don't detest me, Demeter.'

'Why on earth should I ?'

'I'd slipped back to the past again, was pretending to myself that you were a reincarnation of that fruitful goddess, whose love was the love of life. It isn't mine, therefore she would

47

have been my enemy.'

'That's the kind of thing an undergraduate would say; one of the bright young intellectuals who persuade themselves that life is not worth the living, and that death is sweet.'

'You think it's an absurd attitude of mind?'

Her eyes rested on him with amusement, and he said, 'Probably you're right. I doubt if anyone could change you. You walk in the sun, and you always will.'

'It's nice of you to hope so.'

'Did I say it was what I hoped?'

'It's what you implied.'

'Perhaps I did. Well, more than once I've been — er — enabled to give people their heart's desire. Not an impossibility when one has money, influential friends, a certain amount of power. But in your case, you'll probably work out your own destiny.'

'You certainly couldn't help me to achieve my heart's desire,' Clare said with a faint sigh. 'Nobody could.'

'Is it such an impossible one?'

'Not in the least impossible.' As she spoke Clare cocked her head to a listening attitude and said, 'Geoff has stopped working, so we're free to disturb him. He's been working for hours, and is probably ravenous. Will you stay for lunch? I shall have to cook it myself, for there's a fair at Portmerron, and I gave Joan and Cook the day off. Barbara is still only fit for very light work, and the dailies are hopeless.'

Nichol said, 'Perhaps I can help you. I'm not a bad cook, and sometimes take over from Links, who hasn't an idea above fried chops and steamed pudding. Now if you've any mushrooms . . .'

'How did you know?'

'I heard you say the other day that you often got up early on a fine morning to gather them, and this morning was exceptionally fine.'

'Well, I did, and the trawlers were out late last night, and had a good catch, so there's fish. None of us cares for steamed pudding, but Cook made a mousse with cherries and nuts and Madeira in it, before she left this morning. Angela hasn't much appetite, but I thought she would like that.'

'From the sound of it, she'll be hard to please if she doesn't.'

'Barbara will already have taken her her lunch,' Clare said, 'and Geoff will give me a hand, but I can use you as well.'

'You'll be surprised at my efficiency. I'm only sorry Angela isn't well enough to join us.'

Geoffrey entered on the last words and said cheerfully, 'She soon will be. I haven't seen her and I'm curious. She must be an intriguing young woman.'

'Nichol tells me they are old friends,' said Clare. 'He doesn't think it was an amazing coincidence that he was the one to find her washed up on the rocks, but I do.'

Geoffrey, questioning Nichol about this incident, did not seem to find it extraordinary. It was Angela's history which was fantastic.

Her career as a provincial actress had been undistinguished, but her chance meeting with the Indian prince when he was visiting a historically interesting old city in the North of England, where Angela was appearing at the local theatre, and his instant attraction to her, had been romantic in the extreme, especially when followed by a speedy wedding and then divorce.

'If she had been a blonde beauty, it would have been understandable,' Geoffrey said, 'but from her pictures she was a thin, wispy little thing, with a brown skin and no particular beauty.'

'Her eyes are remarkable,' said Clare, 'and she has personality. When we toured together, she made me more than half believe that she had second sight.'

'She has,' Nichol said.

'You have evidence of it?' Geoffrey's raised brows were incredulous.

'I have. It's a gift, though some people might not think it enviable. Angela's mother was a Spaniard, and when I was in Spain a few months ago, I had sufficient curiosity to make enquiries about her family. She had told me her mother's maiden name, which was once an illustrious one, therefore it wasn't difficult to delve into past history. In Seville, in the time of Ferdinand and Isabella, an ancestress of Angela's was accused of being in league with the devil. She was tried for sorcery and burned. After that, the great family of which she was a member, were disgraced, and they gradually sank lower in the social scale. Angela's mother was a member of an itinerant band of players at the time when her father met her and married her.'

'And you think Angela has inherited the gifts of her ancestress?' Geoffrey enquired.

'Possibly. Also her father was a Scot, and they as a race have psychic gifts.'

'An uncomfortable girl to marry, if one believed in such a heritage. I wonder if the Maharajah . . .'

Nichol was smiling. 'From all I heard, and not only from Angela, I gather he was in awe of her. Like most of his race he's superstitious, and when Angela demanded a divorce, he did not refuse her.'

'He probably thought he was well out of such a marriage, whatever the lady's charms.'

Clare interrupted, saying vehemently, 'Oh, do stop this ridiculous talk. I don't believe a word of it. I like Angela. Naturally such a marriage wouldn't work out. I hope she'll start again and be normal and happy. But nothing seems normal just now . . . the storm itself wasn't normal . . . and that beastly cottage ought to be pulled down. Atmosphere is an overworked word, but there's something in the air these days which makes us all strange and unnatural.'

'Darling, you imagine it,' said Geoffrey.

'I don't. Even your music sounded different this morning.'

'Why not? I'm working on something different.'

'Strange, wild, frightening,' said Clare. 'I love your songs and dance music. Why should you think it beneath you to please people such as I?'

'I'd be a fool if I did, but even you with your passion for the normal must admit it's normal for any creative person to yearn to get off the beaten track now and then. But I dare say we have become a bit morbid lately, and I agree Nichol shouldn't be living in that abominable cottage. Why not pack up, and come here for a few weeks? Clare and I would be relieved if you did.'

Nichol turned his dark, bright eyes upon Clare. 'Would you, Demeter?'

'Certainly.'

'Why Demeter?' asked Geoffrey.

Clare answered impatiently, 'It's nonsense. He pretends he believes in reincarnation, and says that I'm the reincarnation of the Earth-Mother.'

'That was Ceres.'

'Demeter was one of her other names – the Greek version I think.'

'It's not a bad simile,' Geoffrey allowed. 'I can't remember having seen a picture of Ceres, but if an artist wanted a model for her, he couldn't choose a better one.'

Clare, uneasily conscious of the appraising glance of both men, moved restlessly. She waited for Geoffrey to repeat his invitation. When he did, Nichol refused it.

'It's very decent of you,' he said, 'but I'm not alone at the cottage. As you know, I have Links, who's a mixture of valet and cook.'

'Bring him along too, there's room for both of you in the theatre wing,' said Geoffrey.

Clare felt her throat constrict. She had the curious and unpleasant feeling that Nichol could read her mind, would discover her reluctance to have him as a guest. She moved away and, on the pretence of changing the arrangement of some flowers in the vase, contrived to stand behind him, out of his immediate range of vision.

'No, really,' he said easily. 'I'm not sensitive to what Clare calls atmosphere, and I'm comfortable enough at the cottage. Links is as tough as I, and between us we've made the place cheerful; changed it around to some extent. I've had various belongings sent along which I've collected while travelling.'

Clare repressed a sigh of relief at this definite refusal. But feeling guilty of inhospitality, she said : 'If anything unpleasant should happen, I hope you'll change your mind.'

'I promise you I will,' Nichol answered readily, and then added : 'But there's one thing you *can* do for me, if you will – and you can think of it as laying a ghost – come along in a body to a party I'm planning to give. It'll be a buffet party –

51

the easiest type for a bachelor to organize.'

'Do you really mean all of us, including Becky and her wheel-chair?' Geoffrey asked.

'Certainly.'

'Then it'll be some party.'

'I shall also ask Dr Irris and his delightful wife. Mrs Irris is shudderingly fascinated at the thought of stepping over the macabre threshold. Then there's the Vicar, who has called – nice chap who prides himself on being so broad-minded and secular that he's succeeded in practically smothering the cleric – and there's Frecell, the bank manager . . .'

'A rout indeed,' Geoffrey observed.

Nichol turned about to glance at Clare, still occupied with her flower arrangement. 'Can you face up to it?' he asked.

'Oh yes. I dare say I shall feel as Mrs Irris feels – shudderingly fascinated.'

'Good. Then I shall start to make arrangements, and let you know the day.'

'Meanwhile,' Geoffrey said, glancing at the clock, 'it's past one and I'm ravenous. What about lunch, darling?'

'You're both roped in to help me cook it,' she said.

*

Angela was sitting by the fire in her bedroom, supported by many cushions, and with a rug over her knees, when Clare visited her during the afternoon.

'Did Dr Irris say you could sit up?' she asked.

'He did, and tomorrow I can come downstairs. I'm glad to see you, Clare. There's much to say, but I haven't felt up to it. I want to thank you.'

'Please don't!' Clare sat down near to her. 'We're all thankful – I've been especially thankful as we were friends. When you were brought here, and we knew you would live, I wanted to cry with joy. We'd felt dreadful at our helplessness to save the poor people on the ship. Our only hope was that the sea was so rough, they must have been too ill to care . . .'

'Most of them were dreadfully seasick,' Angela said.

'Don't talk of it, or remember it if it hurts too much.'

Angela's vivid blue eyes, larger than ever now, because her

face was thin, were filmed by tears, but they did not fall. She said, 'I can't stop remembering. Could you?'

'No.'

'But it doesn't do any good to talk about it, and actually I don't remember any of the last part – how it was I came to be on the raft – drifting on the sea . . . perhaps I was knocked unconscious.'

'Yes – perhaps.'

'I've been here a week,' said Angela, 'and you've been so good to me. It must have been a frightful upset for you.'

'As though I minded.'

'I'm sure you didn't. I'm sure you were glad, as you say. You were always such a dear. I was fond of you.'

'So was I of you, Angela.'

'What an awful tour that was – a stupid play, and I had scarcely anything to do in it, and nobody liked me, except you. They were all sure I should bring them bad luck.'

'Did you know that? You never said.'

'Of course I knew – but I didn't mind; it was rather amusing to have everyone scared of me. But you weren't. I hadn't the evil eye for you, whatever I had for anyone else.'

'Such rubbish. You were putting on an act.'

'I dare say I was. Clare, I wish we hadn't drifted apart.'

'That wasn't deliberate – people do. I married and lived in London, and you married too. I read about it, of course, and I did think of writing to you then to wish you luck.'

'Well, I had luck,' Angela said. 'I knew it couldn't last, but it was all wildly exciting. Suddenly I was living in a story out of *The Arabian Nights* – jewels and furs and the villa at Cannes, and masses of servants. I used to clap my hands, for the pleasure of seeing them come running.'

'Native servants?' Clare asked, smiling because Angela spoke as a child might have spoken.

'Oh yes, all of them. Selim wouldn't have white servants. They feared and hated me and thought me a witch. That was fun too. They, none of them, not Selim's secretary, or any of his hangers-on who were in exile with him, could imagine what he saw in me. I wasn't even pretty. He said it was my eyes. I fascinated him – there was something about me which was

53

more important to him than beauty. But finally people persuaded him I was trying to poison him; that I had nothing to gain by staying with him, because he had settled so much money on me. I became terribly tired of the Oriental set-up, so I told Selim I wanted a divorce and it would be the worse for him if he didn't give me one, and he was glad to let me go, because by that time he couldn't enjoy a thing he ate, for fear I'd put poison in it.'

'Is that supposed to be funny, or isn't it?'

'It isn't funny – not really, because he was horribly scared. I played it up. Nichol Nairn knew all about it. But I don't want to talk about Nichol.'

'You might have died as a result of all you've gone through, if he hadn't found you. To me it seems amazing that it should have been somebody you knew.'

'He's an amazing person,' said Angela.

'Is he? It's my belief he puts on an act, just as you did. He's mischievous, but harmless. I like him. We all like him.'

'If he meant you to like him, then you would,' Angela said in a sombre voice.

'But it would be difficult not to. He's full of clever talk, but underneath he's simple. That's rather engaging, don't you think?'

'Simple! Nichol?'

'Well, that's how he impresses me. Cook and Joan are out today, so Geoff and Nichol and I cooked the lunch, but Nichol did most of it. I was astonished at the professional way in which he went about it. He did what I believe Americans call a deep fry . . .'

She broke off for Angela had uttered a choked exclamation, and then she laughed. 'A deep fry!' she repeated.

'Why not? Lots of men are chefs, and Nichol seems to have a gift for cooking. I don't usually use oil, but he insisted, and Geoff said it was a long time since he'd eaten fish and mushrooms which tasted so good.'

'You don't know how funny that sounds,' gasped Angela, wiping the tears from her eyes. 'Funny – and yet not a bit funny.'

'I can't see the joke myself.'

54

'You wouldn't.' And then becoming serious, Angela said :
'I like you, and perhaps he does too, if he can like anyone; but
we're not your sort, and the sooner we get out of here the
better.'

'Nichol isn't staying here, and please don't go, Angela, not
yet, not until you're quite fit. You look awfully tired and
frail. Besides, it's lovely for me to have a friend of my own
here, somebody young.'

'Your husband is young, isn't he, and that girl who has
helped to look after me? She's more than an ordinary maid.
She says you played together as children.'

'So we did, and I'm fond of Joan, but it isn't quite like
having a friend. As for Geoffrey, I don't see nearly enough of
him. He composes music, and he has to be alone for that, and
when he's in the mood he works for hours. He's in the mood
just now. Anyway you can't go until you have some new
clothes. All you had on board was lost, and things of mine
would wrap twice round you.'

Angela said, 'I've made out a list and sent it to a shop
in London where I have an account. There ought to be large
boxes arriving any day.'

'What fun! Can I help you choose? Will you feel fit to
try on clothes?'

'Of course I shall. It still seems strange to think I've money
to buy anything I fancy. All the same, I grieve for some
of my furs which I had with me. They were really marvellous
– and there were jewels, too . . .'

'I suppose there'll be compensation from the shipping
people,' Clare said, 'And at least that gorgeous emerald ring
was still on your finger.'

'That was lucky. It was always tight for me.'

'Even if you couldn't replace what you've lost, it would be
a small thing in comparison with your life. It's that which
matters.'

Angela agreed. 'It mattered terribly to me – to live; you'll
not believe me perhaps, but when I realized we were all in
danger, I was more angry than frightened. I saw everything
being torn away from me, just as I was free . . .'

'But you'd been free for months – . . . even before your

divorce. You'd left the Maharajah some time before then.'

'Yes, but I was ill. I was in a clinic in Paris, and then I went home to Ireland for a holiday, and I made such plans there.'

'Were you seriously ill?'

Angela hesitated and then said : 'I've not told you all that happened between Selim and me. There were frightful scenes, I had so many enemies. He wanted to keep me with him at first, and they – the men who had been his advisers when he was in power – persuaded him there was only one way . . . to keep me in purdah as though I were a woman of his own race. Then I should be harmless, they said. Selim listened to them and tried to do just that. I was terrified – horrified – but he had to let me go at last because I said I'd put a curse on him, and that he would die. He began to get ill, and although I was shut up and couldn't hurt him, he thought that by witchcraft I was slowly killing him. Finally he was glad to see the last of me. But I had had a bad time too, imprisoned in a suite of rooms with servants who waited on me, but were like warders. I mattered nothing to them, I was only the white woman who had found favour in their master's eyes. I'd been fascinated by Selim in the beginning, for he was handsome and romantic, and he gave me wonderful things. I was flattered, too, because he was crazy about me. But Clare – you can't imagine . . . to be massaged and scented by those slaves, for they were nothing more, just to wait for him to visit me, and to make love . . . In the end I loathed him, and the only thing I could do was to make him believe I could kill him – by suggestion. But it took it out of me; by the time he was frightened enough to set me free and agree to a divorce, I was nearly out of my mind. I had a bad nervous breakdown and wasn't fit for anything for weeks.'

'But couldn't you have got in touch with any of your friends?'

'How? When I was a prisoner? And afterwards – well, I was only thankful I need never see him again.'

'Does Nichol know about this?'

Once again Angela hesitated. 'I don't suppose he would mind me telling you,' she said at last. 'He was the one person who helped me during those weeks when I was a prisoner. We had been friendly, and he wondered what had become of me. He bribed one of the servants, who told him the truth, and then he sent me a note, which the woman managed to give me. Wrapped up in the paper was a queer charm; a little gold disc with signs on it. I could make nothing of them, but in his note Nichol told me that my one chance was to play on Selim's superstitious fears. I was to hold the charm in my hand and wish and wish that he would become sick and thin and frightened, and I must tell him what I was doing. He couldn't dare to try to take the charm away, for the touch of it would kill him instantly.'

'Did he really believe it – a man who had been educated at Eton and Cambridge?' Clare asked incredulously.

'Education doesn't go deep with such a man as Selim. Yes, he believed it – or at least he didn't disbelieve sufficiently to take the risk. Nichol knew as much – he's clever.'

'Well, it seems to me it would have been better to have gone to the British Consul and told him how you were being treated. Surely the Embassy would have taken action?'

'I don't know – there'd have been a lot of red tape, and Selim and his friends were cunning. They might have said I was mad or something.'

'I only wonder you weren't driven out of your mind.'

'I nearly was. Do you wonder that, when I was in fear of drowning, I was furiously angry? I felt cheated. I'd have done anything . . . given half my fortune for a chance to live . . . given my very soul . . . wouldn't any girl have felt the same – wouldn't you?'

'I don't know. Yes, I suppose so.'

'I know what you're thinking,' Angela said accusingly. 'You're sure you could never have done what I did; married an Indian prince for his wealth, and then have half-killed the poor wretch by terrifying him. But you've had a very different kind of life. You were on tour with me, but you could have left when you liked. You had your home to go to, and your uncle who was famous. I was still poor and unknown and struggling to live, when you met Geoffrey Deering and married him. Everything has come easily to you, but I've had

57

to scrape along, and when I saw my chance, I took it.'

'Angela, I'm not blaming you.' Clare spoke gently. 'It's true I've been lucky. How can I say what I should have done in your place? But why be so bitter, now? Every other woman on the boat was drowned, but you have been saved. You're young and you can have a wonderful life. You won't be friendless any longer, and with so much money you can do a lot of good.'

'Sit on committees?' queried Angela. 'I doubt if I'm the type.'

'I hadn't thought of anything definite – but it's wonderful to be able to give people fun – especially children, even if it is only treating a dozen or so to ice-cream.'

'Well, that certainly won't break me,' Angela said, 'though I'm not fond of children. To be honest, my main idea is to give myself a good time while I'm young and can enjoy life; though I shall do my best to live to be old, very old. Won't you?'

'I'm not sure. I see enough of old age here. It isn't much fun.'

'It's better than being dead,' said Angela.

4

A quantity of dress boxes arrived from London. Angela had accounts at several shops, she had ordered lavishly, and all the women at 'Welcomes' shared in the excitement when the boxes were unpacked, with the exception of Becky, who shrugged her shoulders and said she had seen too many beautiful stage costumes in her day to be interested in anything less than Worth.

But Clare, Phillis and Marty collected in Angela's bedroom, and sat around in a semi-circle while she, with Joan's aid, tried on one garment after another. There were hats also, and on the bed a pile of lingerie and gloves and shoes.

Phillis, watching rapturously as Angela twisted and turned before them, said it was as good as a private mannequin show, and she was thrilled when Angela presented her with a pale blue satin stole, lined with shell pink velvet, and bordered with rhinestones; an extravagantly beautiful wrap such as Phillis adored.

Angela decided to keep several items. 'They will do until I can have some clothes designed for me,' she said.

Clare remembered her as she had been only five years ago; a shabby, unknown actress, wearing cheap dresses and an ulster. Now she had bought several hundred pounds' worth as casually as she would have once bought a quarter of a pound of boiled sweets.

Phillis, twittering with pleasure over her stole, helped to stow the clothes away in the wardrobe. Marty undertook to repack those things which were to be returned to the shops. Joan suggested that Angela had had an exhausting two hours and should rest.

But Angela spent most of the remainder of the day making alterations to clothes which she would want to wear in the near future. Phillis, always deft with her needle, offered to help. Joan remarked that Geoffrey had been shut up in the garden-room for hours, had eaten only a sandwich for his lunch which he had asked to be brought to him there, and didn't Mrs Deering think that somebody ought to go in and interrupt him?

Clare, mindful of how much Geoffrey hated to be disturbed when he was working, said doubtfully that she supposed she ought to remind him that it was past the tea hour, and Joan said that in that case she would get a tray ready and carry it in.

'Never have I known him to work for such hours,' Joan said, 'and the queerest music – the sort that gives you the creeps.'

'How possessive that girl is about your husband,' Angela said lightly as Joan went out of the room. 'She more or less tells you how to treat him.'

It was the first time this had actually struck Clare, but now it came to her that it was true enough, and Phillis piped

59

up to say: 'Oh, she's a very bossy girl. I've always thought so. Useful though she is, if I were in your shoes, I don't think I could put up with it.'

'It doesn't mean anything,' Clare said defensively. 'Joan has looked after us since we were first married, and we were such an erratic pair, both of us working so hard, Geoff at his music and I on the stage, that she had to take a firm stand.'

'All the same,' Phillis said, when she was alone with Angela, 'I shouldn't like it, if I were Clare. Don't think I'm a nasty-minded old woman, dear, for I'm very slow to believe evil of anyone, but I've had a suspicion once or twice that Joan is fonder of Geoff than she should be.'

'But that often happens with housekeepers,' Angela said. 'They fuss over a man, though the mistress of the house can look out for herself. Clare is a darling, and a man lucky enough to be loved by her wouldn't look twice at anyone else.'

'Oh, my dear, of course,' Phillis eagerly assented, 'but all the same I've a strong suspicion that Joan, for all her quiet ways, is one for the men. She's deep.'

Angela changed the conversation by saying, 'I sent for a necklace for Clare which I saw advertised, but I didn't give it to her when everyone else was there; I dare say she'll make a fuss about accepting it, though I shall insist. Would you like to see it?'

Phillis exclaimed with admiration when the delicate gold chain, studded with semi-precious stones was revealed; turquoise matrix; moonstones; chrysoprase. It was exquisite, Phillis gushed, and there were also presents for the men, of cigarette-cases in leather, embossed with gold monograms, and for Becky a set of cut-glass liqueur glasses, Barbara and Cook and even Mrs Marsh and Adelaide, the two dailies, had had been remembered, for there were embroidered handkerchiefs for all of them.

'Surely these are not parting gifts, dear Angela?' Phillis said. 'I know Clare hopes to keep you here with us for a long time yet.'

But Angela said this was unlikely, now that she was starting to get about again. She intended writing to house agents in Mayfair to tell them to look out for a suitable small house for her.

*

Two days later, Nichol and Angela met.

Although he had bided his time, she had known it was impossible to avoid a meeting for much longer. She would gladly have departed unobtrusively, and left it to Nichol to follow her to London, but knowing there was not one member of the household who would not have thought this extraordinary, she lacked the courage to take the decisive step.

Besides, it wouldn't make all that difference, she thought despondently. She would hate and dread seeing him wherever it might be. The fact that she was wearing an extremely becoming dove-grey dress, with a tiny waist and enormous leg-of-mutton sleeves, helped to enhance her morale.

'You look very well,' Nichol said, when he arrived to find her alone in the living-room, Clare having deliberately arranged that the meeting should take place without onlookers. 'You silly girl, you could have seen me long ago.'

'I couldn't. I had no clothes to wear until the day before yesterday.'

She did not offer to shake hands, he did not seem to expect it, but said quietly: 'No sense in dashing yourself against the bars.'

'You use very hackneyed similes,' said Angela tartly.

'The coin of the country, my dear. Come sit down, relax. This enmity is absurd. It's you who are in my debt, not I in yours.'

'What do you want from me?'

'Nothing very difficult for you to deliver; but it's as well for you to understand the position. You were – er – quite naturally in a somewhat demoralized state when we made our bargain, though you knew what you were doing.'

'I'm not denying it, am I?'

'Because it would be useless. But as a matter of curiosity, I should be interested to know if you regret your decision.'

'I thought you knew everything – even my thoughts.'

'With some slight exertion I can discover them, but I'm in a lazy mood this morning. Come, tell me.'

'I don't regret it,' she said sullenly. 'Given the same offer, I should make the same choice.'

'Good! It's much more pleasant when there's satisfaction on both sides.'

Angela's hands were clenched on her lap. She looked down at them, fighting for composure, but her voice trembled as she asked: 'How long have I got?'

'My dear girl, that depends upon how useful you are to me.'

'I see.'

'You should find the work interesting, and it's only a part-time assignment. You'll have plenty of time for parties, theatres, and travel. In fact, the more you travel, the more friends you make, the better.'

'Friends! I shall never be able to have a real friendship again.'

'Had you many in the old days? My information is that you were far from popular.'

'Who informed you, or do you do your own detective work?'

Nichol said, smiling as though amused, 'I suppose you can say I'm self-employed. Those who work for me, do so secretly, and their names are not revealed even to one another. Come now, Angela, I've not been hard on you. I've given you plenty of time to recover from your ordeal, but you've work to do before you leave here.'

'What work? I planned to go by the end of the week.'

'You must stay a little longer than that. There will be no difficulties. Clare has repeatedly said how delighted she is to have you here. The set-up is an interesting one. I've rarely known a family where so many people were walking on tight ropes. I dare say you've discovered that for yourself.'

'They have their little secrets, of course. Who hasn't? But it's all so trivial – not worth your attention, or mine.'

'Let me be the judge of that.'

She sighed heavily, but it was a sigh of resignation rather than rebellion. 'It's hateful. They've all been good to me.'

'Many people will be good to you in the future, but you won't weaken because of it.'

There was a considerable silence. Angela seemed to be considering this. Then she asked, 'Will you always be with me, or shall I work independently of you?'

'You will often appear to work independently of me, but you'll be told how and when to report to me. During this first test, I shall be in direct touch with you. I'm giving a party next week at the cottage I've rented, which everyone in the district holds in superstitious dread. But fear has its attractions, and that and curiosity will bring them along. Before then, I've no doubt you'll have put in some useful spade work. I'll give you a few items of information. Can you memorize them, or would you prefer to take notes?'

'It's safer to memorize,' Angela said, and Nichol nodded approvingly.

'Exactly. Well now, for your information, in that desk over there, a fine old piece, there's a secret drawer which none of the family has yet discovered. I'll show you the trick – how to open it. There's a diary in it, which will be of great interest to Clare.'

'Can't you leave Clare out of it?' Angela cried on a note of genuine pain. 'She's one of the few people in all my life I've really cared about, and from the way in which she spoke about you I thought – though I admit it seems impossible – that you liked her. You're rich and good-looking and fascinating, hosts of people imitate you, admire you, flock round you, but you have little experience of real friendship, such as Clare has for you . . .'

For an instant it seemed to Angela that she had made an impression on him, for a different expression was reflected in the bright, dancing eyes which had been fixed on her in amused malice. If not a softened expression, it was at least a thoughtful one.

'I admit that,' he said, 'and it's the oddest thing – for her kind and mine are traditional enemies. I expected an entirely different reaction – a pricking of the thumbs, in fact.'

'Clare is not a witch,' Angela said. 'She's a kind-hearted and honest person.'

'Exactly – that's why!'

Angela observed bitterly, 'She may be a prototype of the Earth-Mother, but she has no premonition that you are the prototype of a shoal of locusts. But then so far as I can make out, she not only trusts you, but everyone else. That girl, Joan, for instance – you haven't been blind to her potentialities.'

'No.'

'It's natural that Clare should be blind. She told me you called her Demeter, and Joan is her exact opposite; sterile and passionate – the kind of woman Geoffrey Deering would like Clare to be, or imagines he would. He'll fight against it, but . . .'

'Poor fellow, it will be a losing battle,' Nichol said.

'Could you be wrong, or are you infallible?'

'Have I ever said I was infallible? That's for you to discover.'

'This cat and mouse business! It amuses you to give me a glimmer of hope now and again.'

'Let us dismiss your reactions for the moment,' said Nichol. 'There's this nurse factotum. Is she friendly towards you?'

'Very. They all are.'

'Good. She'll be receiving a letter before long – it may be just before my party, or just after it. She will confide in you, if you are clever, and that will mean disaster for Miss Becky Redcliffe. As for the other two . . .'

'The coquettish Phillis with her miserable little vice, old Noel cribbing other people's books to bolster up the biography he thinks he can write and probably never will write – surely they at least are too harmless.'

'Do what you can,' Nichol instructed.

'Have you ever let anyone off?' Angela asked.

'No. It's not my habit to go back on a bargain.'

'But sometimes I only half-believe it,' Angela said wildly. 'I wouldn't believe it for a moment if it were not for all the talks we had in Cannes. It fascinated me then – I was ravished by curiosity.'

'And you never doubted me, or what I could do for you or against you. You would be very stupid to doubt me now. You have had sufficient proof.'

'It will send me out of my mind.'

'Not if you keep your sense of proportion. And if it did – well, most people who knew your ancestress's history would say she was mad. She confessed to the most monstrous, the most fascinating things.'

Angela sighed heavily. 'I was a fool to think that mercy had any meaning for you.'

'Its meaning is weakness,' said Nichol.

*

'Angela is staying for another week or so,' Clare told Geoffrey. 'At first she insisted she must leave almost at once, but later she thought better of it.'

'Probably because of Nichol's party; everyone seems to be excited about it,' Geoffrey said.

Of late they had had little privacy and little opportunity to talk together, for Geoffrey was working for such long hours that he was scarcely seen during the daytime, and at night was too tired for conversation. But this evening he had not departed to the garden-room after the evening meal. His work had gone badly that day and he needed a breathing space.

They had gone to bed early, thankful that it had not been necessary to stay up on Angela's account, for she had complained of a headache and had been willing to make the evening a short one.

As Clare sat before her dressing-table mirror, watching Geoff, listening to him as he pottered about between the bedroom and the bathroom, she was in a soothed, contented mood.

'It would take more than a local party to soothe Angela,' she said, 'and she laughs when people say the cottage is haunted. Of course there's no evidence of it – and she wouldn't think it important anyway. What's to haunt a girl whose ancestress was a witch, and who claims she can foretell the future? If anything it's her line of country.'

Geoffrey laughed. 'I gather you don't believe in Angela's supernatural powers.'

'I wouldn't quite say that.' Clare's face reflected in the mirror was thoughtful. 'I think there is something eerie about her, but it's more than likely there's an explanation for it. Perhaps some people are born with it – I mean with more sensitive antennae than others; they sense divine things

65

more keenly, just as other people might have keener sight or hearing. Today, Angela was admiring that old desk Uncle Quentin always used, and she asked me if it had a secret drawer. I said I had no idea, and then she said she suspected it had, and if I liked she would try to find it. Somehow or other I wasn't too keen, but that seems silly, especially as there might be something of value hidden in it.'

'Always supposing there *is* a secret drawer,' Geoffrey commented. 'I doubt it myself, as I've used the desk a good deal, and we thoroughly overhauled it when you took possession. Probably we'd have stumbled on a secret panel if there had been such a thing. However, there's no harm in letting Angela demonstrate her powers.'

'No, I suppose not.' And then Clare asked : 'Do you like her?'

'I'm not sure. She's an intelligent girl and interesting in some ways, but she's very wrapped up in herself. No, on mature consideration, I'd say I don't like her – particularly. Do you?'

'I thought I did, but now I'm more sorry for her than anything.'

'Why? Most people would say she's a singularly fortunate young woman.'

'Well, if it's fortunate to be haunted, tormented by some private fear, and obviously in a state of constantly tensed nerves . . . if anyone thinks that lashings of cash can make up for that state of mind, yes, then she's lucky, I suppose.'

'It's difficult to like people, isn't it?' Geoffrey said thoughtfully. 'To love is less difficult, to be physically drawn to another human being is all too easy, but liking – that's much rarer. I like you, darling, very much.'

'Do you, Geoff?' Clare wheeled round on the dressing-table stool to look at him. 'And yet these last weeks we've seen so little of each other. It's as though you haven't wanted to see much of me.'

Geoffrey answered lightly, 'That's the way of it when I'm chasing elusive chords. People, even you, are distracting.'

'But I could be with you when you go tearing out of the house to walk for miles . . . I'm as good a walker as you, but

66

you won't have me.'

'Because I'm still working on the darned thing in my head. I walk, but I'm more or less blind to my surroundings.'

'You certainly are. Mrs Irris told me she passed you in the village street the other day, and you stared at her as though you'd never seen her before, and dashed on without a word.'

'Did she? I hope you explained.'

'Oh yes. I said you were in a more or less continuous trance. That you sometimes appeared for meals but quite often didn't, and that Joan frequently had to take you trays of food, plump them on the piano and prompt you to eat about every third mouthful. She seems to be able to do that without irritating you. If I tried to bring you back to earth you'd bellow at me.'

'What a boor I sound,' Geoffrey said remorsefully. 'I'm sorry, darling, but it's true I *am* obsessed when I'm slogging away at something promising.'

'It's the storm which gave you the inspiration for this new thing. I wish it hadn't.'

'But why?'

'It's difficult to explain. There probably isn't an explanation, but nothing has been the same since that night. It's as though we've all got mixed up with something we can't control, which is bigger than ourselves – menacing. And this new music of yours – we've all heard snatches of it – it's frightening . . . not a real storm conveyed through music, but a demoniac onslaught, as though evil beings rode on the waves and in the clouds, as though all the world was given up to fury and terror.'

'That's a very good description.' Geoffrey was impressed. 'And if I've conveyed as much, then I'm on the right road. Wasn't that how the storm seemed to us all?'

'Yes, but if only one could forget it. You are perpetuating it.'

'But if I have this sense of inspiration, shouldn't I be mad to pass it up? I've wasted my time on so much that's trivial.'

'It hasn't been a waste of time. As I've told you over and over again, you've given pleasure to thousands. If the storm

67

music is a success, will it give pleasure?'

'Not in the same way, but if it's good music it will mean something. It will lift people out of themselves, and it may even do good. Don't you insist that to do good should be the primary motive of creative work? It's not negligible to make people aware of the force and majesty of nature; or even to make them wonder if there is something noble beyond the enclosing walls of safety which we try to build around ourselves.'

Clare admitted this was true. She said, 'It would mean a lot to you, I know, if you did make something beyond a popular success.'

'I'm not despising the money angle,' Geoffrey said with a wry smile. 'I'm a slow worker and the money my other music has brought in is erratic, and such work is not too well paid. This storm music may be profitable, as well as a cause for personal satisfaction.'

'But why do you worry about money so much?' Clare protested. 'We have enough.'

'Because of *your* inheritance, darling.'

'It belongs to us both, equally; everything we have belongs to us both.'

'But if this house and the money hadn't been left to you, you'd still have been working on the stage, for I couldn't keep you in decent comfort. I shan't be content until I'm doing well enough to run this house, and then you can squander your own income or not touch it. That's part of my way of being in love with you. Does it seem ridiculous?'

'I understand,' Clare said, 'though it doesn't matter to me . . . and yet in a way it does, because it would be such a pleasure to you. When you are rich and terribly famous, I'll give away all Uncle Quentin's money, if you want me to.'

'I shouldn't want that – nothing so drastic. I'd probably be content if I could buy you a few luxuries which even now you can't afford – diamonds or a sealskin coat, though you'll probably say you want neither.'

'I'd love them and be terribly proud if you gave them to me.' Clare looked at him so sweetly that his heart and senses were both stirred.

68

'I've been neglecting you,' he said.

'You couldn't help it. I know you're scarcely aware that anyone exists when you're really absorbed in your work.'

'Well, I'm not absorbed now, so now's your opportunity to make a fuss of me.'

She smiled as she retorted, 'Why should I want to make a fuss of you?'

'Goodness knows. I'll make a fuss of you instead, shall I?'

He reached for her, pulled her towards him by the skirt of her nightgown, and tipped her backwards on the bed. She lay there, looking up at him with serious eyes as he bent over her.

'Want me?' he asked.

'Yes . . . if . . . Geoff – please . . . just this once couldn't we . . .?'

'Not worth the risk, my sweet.'

'It might not mean – a baby.'

'I've a hunch that it would.'

'Why would it matter so much? It's so cold-blooded this way.'

'There's nothing cold about me, darling.'

He sat down on the bed beside her, taking her head on his knee and smiling down into her eyes. She was passive.

'Why must it be always like this?' he said.

'I never refuse you,' she reminded him.

'Because you'd think that wrong – it's part of your muddled thinking. No refusal, but no giving either. I can take you without reproaches hurled at me, but it's as though I'm a thief . . . stealing something which doesn't belong to me.'

'Don't let's quarrel – not tonight,' Clare pleaded.

'It takes two to make a quarrel and you never do. You're so beautiful, I adore you, though I can't move you even to a slight degree.'

'It's because you cheat.'

'Don't talk such nonsense!'

His hands clenched bruisingly on her arms, but she did not wince. He shook her slightly. 'You're not a cold woman . . . you were happy enough when we were first married – dazed and bewildered perhaps – but still happy. Love could

69

be wonderful between us.'

'Yes – it could,' she whispered. 'Oh, Geoff . . .'

'You deliberately steel yourself against me, because – as yet – I won't consider giving you a child.'

'It's not that – I don't – but I can't help myself. It all seems so pointless . . . a routine . . . frustration for both of us. If it were different – I'd be different, too.'

'But I've explained my reasons, Clare – over and over again I've explained. When we were both working, and our earnings were uncertain it would have been disastrous to start a family. Now you have money, and the house is yours, but I'm still struggling to make my name. I won't bring children into the world unless I can adequately support them, without relying on you. You can call it unreasonable pride . . .'

'I do,' Clare said, 'but it's not only that. You say you love me, and I believe you – but it's not so much the soul and spirit part of me as my body. You can't bear the thought of seeing it change – you don't want to share me.'

'Well, what of it? Theoretically I'm fond of children, but I've no urge to have any of my own, and I've no mind to be loved – biologically.'

'You wouldn't be. I'd love you, as you want to be loved; after I'd stopped having children, or for years in between having them. You'd be their father and really my husband then. Now I'm confused and baffled – I'm deprived.'

'You don't love me,' he accused.

'I do – I do, but it's not a complete love, not a proud and fruitful love.'

He still leaned over her, his hands on her shoulders, pressing her down upon the bed, but now his coldness equalled hers. He said, 'There was a patriarch in the Old Testament who said to his wife : "Am I not more to you than many sons?" '

'I can't remember what his wife replied to that,' Clare retorted, 'but I doubt if it was satisfactory.'

'Doesn't it mean anything to you that your beauty is precious to me?'

'Yes, but I wouldn't be less beautiful for you, Geoff . . . I know it.'

Her voice and her eyes pleaded with him, but with a shrug

70

he released her, stood up and moved away.

'You know how it was with me,' he said. 'My father was a poor man. My mother was sweet and delicate, and my father, to my mind, was a selfish brute who turned her into a slave. She bore him five children. I was the eldest. All my memories of her are hurtful. I loved her and I saw what her life was; at the wash-tub, mending, ironing, cooking, endlessly endeavouring to feed us sufficiently well, to see that we had shoes on our feet and clothes on our backs. Often when it was past midnight she'd still be at the sewing-machine. She was old in her thirties, and ailing. She never had a holiday or a day's pleasure. Then there was an epidemic of scarlet fever and the whole family caught it. The four younger children died of it. I, the strongest, was the only one to survive. A year later my mother also died.'

'Geoff, dear . . .' Clare murmured in distress.

'I've told you all this before,' he said.

'But not in the same way – with such bitterness.'

'It's a bitter memory.'

'Darling, I can't bear to think you had such wretchedness when you were young. I wish I could blot it all out for you.'

'You won't do that by pity. I want you as a lover – not primarily as the mother of my children. Can you wonder that I've no wish to start a family?'

'But it would be different for us,' she pleaded. 'Our circumstances are different.'

But this was an old argument – always fruitless. Geoffrey shrugged himself into his dressing-gown and went to the door. 'After all, I may as well put in another hour at work,' he said.

*

The storm music passed its zenith and drifted into a wailing, plaintive, minor key. Geoffrey laboured over this, jotting down notes, altering them, trying out a bar over and over again.

It was fortunate, he reflected, that nobody except he and Clare and now Angela slept in the main part of the house. If Clare were disturbed that was her own fault, and Angela had probably been asleep for hours. It was to be hoped so, as her room was overhead.

71

Mindful of this, he kept the soft pedal down. Visitors were a nuisance, he thought exasperatedly, for in the ordinary way he could work into the small hours of the morning. As it was, in case he disturbed Angela, he would feel forced to close the piano this side of midnight.

His anger with Clare slowly passed, for now he was exalted, realizing that during the last week he had done the best work of his life. This was music which needed full orchestration to reveal its power and originality, and he had little doubt that it would be considered worthy.

The dying down of the storm was effective, suggesting as it did the aftermath of sorrow, rebellion and rage. The evil forces had been routed, and now there was little but exhaustion, a picking-up of threads, a weary effort to start again.

He poured over the score, making a marginal note every now and again, and then was startled by a voice behind him. 'You must be worn out. I've made some tea and toast.'

The door had opened almost soundlessly, for he had not heard it, and he turned quickly as Joan put down a tray on a table near him.

'I thought everyone had gone to bed long ago,' he said.

'They have. But my window was open, and your music came floating across the garden. The glass door is ajar. Didn't you know?'

'For heaven's sake close it, or the people in the theatre wing will be disturbed.'

'Well, it's not all that late. Everyone was early tonight.'

'I'm sorry I kept you awake,' Geoffrey said formally.

'It didn't matter. Shall I pour you out your tea?'

'Thank you. It was very decent of you to think of it.'

Joan smiled; a mischievous smile, which brought light and animation to her normally contained and handsome face. 'That's exactly what the old people in the theatre wing would say I wasn't,' she said.

He realized then that she was in her dressing-gown, which was of heavy red velvet and cut with the severity of a man's garment. It was open, and beneath it she was wearing a thin silk robe. It unbuttoned at the throat, and showed her smooth neck.

A good-looking girl of about the same age as Clare, she was Clare's antithesis, built on slender lines, with no hint of the voluptuous beauty which so often inflamed and infuriated Geoffrey with its voiceless demand for fulfilment. He knew well enough that Clare had no desire to be a temptation to him, and since he refused her children would have been better pleased had she not been exciting to him.

'That monk-like gown is respectable enough,' he said casually, drinking his tea.

Joan sat down on the arm of a chair opposite to him. She said, 'It would have been rather too obvious if I had floated in, in a silk negligee, but I did let my hair loose.'

Startled, as much by her tone as her words, Geoffrey gazed at her more closely, and realized that her fair hair, long and thick, was falling over her shoulders to her waist. He met her eyes and was silent, conscious of a throbbing intensity between them, aware that he was now seeing her as a new person.

He had never particularly liked her, though she had been part of his life and Clare's for the last three years, and extremely useful to them. Occasionally he had thought her too dominating.

Now he realized that for reasons best known to herself, Joan had come out into the open. There was unveiled sensuality in her gaze as it met his. It transformed her quiet face.

'You'd better be getting back to bed,' he said with a reluctance which dismayed him.

'Not yet. I've waited so long.'

'Joan – do as I tell you.'

'I would, if you really wanted me to go – but you don't.'

She threw off her dressing-gown, and came close to him. She slid her arm round his neck, and then as he did not immediately repulse her, she put her lips to his in a kiss so long, so lascivious that he gasped.

'Good God!' he said, when he could release himself. 'What's come to you?'

'It was always there, but I've had to hide it. I'd have hidden it for ever if she made you happy, but I know she doesn't – all that lusciousness, and yet nothing.'

She was in his arms now, which involuntarily closed round her, and he realized with delight that there was allure in the slender tautness of a body which only waited for a word or a touch to relax.

He strove to master himself, to end the episode before it developed further, but he could find no words which would not sound hypocritical or pompous.

'You know you need me,' Joan whispered, 'and I need you. I've been crazy about you from the first. It won't hurt her – I don't want to hurt her – she'll get you back if she wants you, and I'll not make trouble.' And then in a breathless whisper: 'I swear I won't make any claim on you or even remind you . . .'

With an effort Geoffrey put her away from him, held her off at arm's length to look at her. He said, 'Clare has known you all her life, you've lived with us and worked with us for years – without a sign. Then why . . .?'

'Because I knew that tonight I'd get my chance with you – if you came back to your music, if you didn't stay with her. I saw your face, how you looked at her, and when you went up the stairs together you were hand in hand . . . and then half an hour or less and you were back here and I heard you playing, and knew she wasn't any good to you, or you to her. Do you think I've lived in the same house for years and not known it? Then why shouldn't I take what she cares nothing for?'

'So you *are* a dark horse after all.'

Joan laughed, and the sound was so new, so strange, so curiously fascinating to Geoffrey that he realized he could never before have heard her laugh. 'It's likely I am,' she said, 'the horse nobody has heard of, until he wins the big race.'

'What makes you think you care for me?'

'You're a man – and strong – why shouldn't I fancy you?'

The answer was so simple, so primitive, that Geoffrey was bewildered afresh, as he thought of her fastidious ways; her immaculate tidiness, the smooth hair with never a strand out of place; the perfection of her cooking, her needlework, all her housewifely services. Yet here she was, a bacchante with

74

her streaming hair, and invitation on her lips and in her eyes.

'I'll be the same as ever tomorrow,' she promised him. 'When I bring you and her your early tea, you'll wonder if it really was between us, and that's the way it's best for it to be. Then nobody will get hurt.'

'I wonder!'

Joan sighed impatiently. 'All this talk, and so little time . . . why can't you trust me?'

He had wanted passion, and Clare had refused him. He had wanted a woman as a lover rather than as a wife, and now a woman, who was as lithe and unrestrained as an animal, was in his arms. With her hungry mouth moving across his cheek she said softly, 'I've given you a shock – you can't make yourself believe it, but you were slow . . . I couldn't make you understand; slower than other men.'

'There *have* been others then?'

'You wouldn't expect me to wait for you, when I wasn't even sure of getting you? Every so often when I've seen a fellow I liked . . .'

Geoffrey couldn't be sure which was the stronger, his fascination or his repulsion. It was extraordinary to think of the mask she had worn so successfully.

'Don't think I'm not fond of her, I am.' Joan said. 'But she doesn't come into this. I wouldn't want her to know . . . I was scared when she asked me if I'd like to leave and go to Mrs Moore, thinking that someone had told her, or that she suspected.'

Geoffrey remembered the morning after the storm, when Clare had made her innocently benevolent suggestion, and Joan had rejected it. And now her face rose before him, and came between him and the face of this strange girl, upturned upon his shoulder.

Resolution strengthened, and as Joan whispered to him, he heard a door open, and footsteps overhead. Joan heard them too, and she sprang away from him. 'That's Miss Rose,' she gasped. 'She's coming downstairs.'

'Go by the window, cut across the garden,' Geoffrey directed.

But Joan, for a moment aghast, quickly recovered. 'No, I'll stay,' she said. 'Why not? I heard you playing – I brought you tea.'

Before Geoffrey's astonished eyes she was making lightning swift changes to her appearance; knotting up the fair hair, pulling her dressing-gown and tightly girdling it at the waist.

As the door handle turned, she ran to open the door, and exclaimed to see Angela on the threshold.

'Miss Rose! Is anything wrong?'

Angela was fully clad, in the dark, silk, ankle-length dress she had worn that evening, but her hair was tumbled and her face white.

'I'm sorry,' she said. 'I fell asleep in my chair before the fire and I had a ghastly sort of dream, though I can't properly remember it now, and when I woke up the fire was out and I was cold and frightened, and I thought I heard voices, and so I came downstairs to see.'

Geoffrey marvelled to hear Joan say soothingly, and as though her presence there was the most natural thing in the world, 'Come along in, and get warm by the fire, miss. Oh dear, how cold you are, and shaking. Lucky I made tea for Mr Deering – it's still hot as I put the cosy over the teapot, and I'll fetch another cup for you. I heard him playing, you see, and it wasn't so late, but I thought he'd be glad of some tea, so I just got up and went to the kitchen and made it.'

Angela accepted the explanation without question. She sat down in the big chair by the fire which was still glowing, and said gratefully that there was nothing she would like better than a cup of tea. As she took it from Joan's hand, she smiled at her. It was as though she sensed nothing in the least unusual in the situation.

Geoffrey, at first doubtful of this, finally decided that no suspicion was aroused, and his manner which had been stilted became natural. Joan said, 'What about a sandwich?' and went off to cut some.

5

'It may take a little time, but I'm sure there *is* a hidden drawer, and that I can find it,' said Angela.

Before an interested audience, consisting of Geoffrey, Clare and the three occupants of the theatre wing, she was exploring the Georgian writing desk in the living-room.

With Clare's permission, she had taken all the papers out of the pigeon-holes and the row of small drawers beneath them. She had tapped with a brass paper-knife, and had listened intently for any hollow sound. Her slim fingers had slid over every inch of the wood, searching for some projection or tiny knob. So far there had been no result, and Geoffrey said with good-humoured indifference, 'You can't be sure. I know many of these old desks have hiding places, but it's not a universal rule, and I made a thorough investigation myself some months ago.'

'But I've seen it,' Angela said. 'Oh, not with my everyday eyes, but with – well, I can only explain it, by saying that I often do see things in my mind. I know there's a secret cavity, and I know that inside there's a book bound in green leather.'

Phillis shivered delicately. 'Oh dear, you sound really uncanny . . . I hope you're not serious.'

'I'm perfectly serious, Miss Gage.' Angela spoke with a gentle voice. 'But there's nothing to be frightened of. There are many more people with "the sight" than you can imagine, and it only means they have six senses instead of the usual five.'

'But that *is* frightening,' Phillis insisted.

Becky said sarcastically, 'Well, the "sight" seems to have let you down today. I should think you've prodded and

77

tapped that desk enough, and might as well put back all the papers.'

'Not just yet. Is there a magnifying glass anywhere?'

'Oh yes, I have one,' Phillis said. 'My sight is good, and I don't need spectacles, but sometimes when print is very small or people write a difficult hand, I find it handy. It's in my room, on the table by my bed.'

'Ring for Marty. She'll fetch it,' said Becky.

Peering through the glass, Angela carefully scanned the woodwork of the small drawers beneath the pigeon-holes, and suddenly she uttered a pleased exclamation.

'I think I have it! Each drawer has a tiny pearl stud which, when pressed, opens it, but this third drawer has a stud which is larger than the others, and although when you press it, it opens just as the others do, it's a trifle stiff. Now, if instead of pressing it, I push it to the left or right . . . Ah, I thought so!'

'Oh, good gracious,' twittered Phillis, for under pressure the entire drawer lifted upwards, revealing a second cavity beneath it.

'It's a double drawer,' Noel said, 'made like a jewel case or dressing-table with a false bottom. Very neat.'

'What about the hidden book? The drawer's empty,' scoffed Becky.

'No, there's something in it. It goes back a long way,' and Angela, plunging in her hand, brought forth a narrow book bound in green leather. 'It's a diary,' she said, as she flicked through the leaves.

'Let me see.' Clare held out her hand, and Angela gave her the book.

Against her will, Becky was impressed, and Phillis giggled hysterically.

'Very unpleasant gift to have, if it is a gift – "the sight", I mean,' Becky said, 'but I suppose it could be useful, especially in the way of finding lost property. Isabel's pearls, for instance, Noel.'

Noel replied in a constrained voice, 'I should scarcely think Angela's second sight would penetrate across the Atlantic.'

78

'But there's a chance that the pearls left New York.'

'I'm convinced they did nothing of the kind.'

'It's quite a story, Angela,' Becky said, settling down with enjoyment to tell it. 'When Noel's wife died, she left him the income from a trust fund and a collection of jade, none of it tremendously valuable, but quite nice to possess. It was only after Noel left America and had settled here that her pearl necklace, which was worth thousands, was discovered to be missing. The pearls had been bequeathed to a niece of Isabel's, and naturally she was in a state when they couldn't be found. She wrote a most unpleasant letter to Quentin, not to Noel – and Quentin was very indignant. Naturally poor Noel was not to blame. For, as he says, Isabel was constantly changing her servants, and was not nearly particular enough about their references.'

'She rarely wore the pearls,' Noel added. 'They could have vanished months before her death. As it was, somebody had replaced them in her jewel-box with a string of imitation ones. The insurance company paid up eventually, so Kate, Isabel's niece, had nothing of which to complain.'

'But before then the best detectives in New York were trying to trace the necklace, and although they tracked down everyone who had worked for Isabel, they couldn't pin the theft on anyone. The pearls have never been traced.'

'Nor will be,' Noel said. 'No doubt the necklace has been broken up and the pearls sold separately.'

He was obviously disturbed by the conversation and Angela said soothingly, 'My second sight wouldn't be of any assistance to you in such a matter. The necklace was lost too long ago and too far away. Besides, I usually foresee the future, not past.' And then she added : 'I adore jade, though, and I would love to see your collection. Will you show it to me before I leave?'

'With pleasure,' Noel said courteously. 'There are some pretty pieces though, as Becky says, nothing outstandingly valuable. I have a small display cabinet in my room. One day I shall sell the stuff. That is, if I find a likely buyer.'

Clare, oblivious of the conversation, was glancing at the first page of the diary. 'It's Uncle Quentin's,' she said, 'a kind of running commentary of his life twenty-six years ago. The date is 1870. I wonder if I ought to keep it.'

'Why not?' Geoffrey said.

'Well, a diary is a private thing, but I don't suppose Uncle Quentin had many secrets, and it seems mainly a record of the parts he played and his social engagements that year. He describes his first appearance in a production of *Othello*. The one and only time he played the part, though he made such a success of it. Perhaps it should be kept, as a record.'

'There's no question about that,' Noel said emphatically. 'It may be of the greatest help in writing his biography. You'd better hand it over to me. I'm the proper person to sift the grain from the chaff.'

'I'd like to skim through it first. I'll do so this afternoon, probably, and then if there's anything likely to be useful to you, I'll let you know.'

'My dear girl, surely I'm the best judge of what will be useful or otherwise.'

'You can decide about that when I've read it, Uncle Noel,' said Clare with unusual obstinacy. 'That is, if I consider the contents should be publicized.'

Geoffrey intervened. 'Clare is right. The diary can only be used with her permission. It may be too personal to be seen by anyone else.'

'Oh really, Geoff,' Phillis said with her airy, empty little laugh, 'one might think you expected to discover that dear Quentin had committed a murder, whereas we all know he had the most noble character, and could have written nothing about himself or his life which would not be uplifting.'

At this, Becky gave vent to a derisive snort. 'Was the poor man that dull? I wouldn't have said so. He had a kind heart, masses of charm and talent, but he must have had his secrets like everyone else. As he made Clare his heiress, it's her business to vet the diary – it's necessary also, for he was at considerable pains to hide it, which suggests it was more than just a record of his professional life.'

Angela disagreed. 'I don't see why, Miss Redcliffe. Discovering one's desk had a secret drawer, wouldn't it be one's impulse to use it? What would be the good of having such a fascinating thing if you didn't hide something in it? A diary is what you would expect to find. It would have been more exciting had it been the missing pearls.'

Becky laughed delightedly. 'That's a fact. Then we should have had cause for speculation. It would have meant that Noel smuggled them over here, that he took Quentin into his confidence, and that they had become partners in crime.'

'You'd better be careful what you say, Becky.' Noel was ruffled. 'That's a most libellous suggestion.'

'My dear man, don't be a fool. How can it be libellous when the pearls were not in the drawer? Where's the harm in my flight of fancy?'

Noel was silent.

*

Late that afternoon Geoffrey, in search of Clare, found her in her bedroom, curled up on the day-bed with the electric fire close to her for warmth. It was a mild day, but when he came over to Clare, and lightly touched her hand, he found it was icy.

'My dear girl, what on earth's the matter – are you ill?' he asked anxiously.

She looked at him dazedly. 'No – I don't think so – but I've had a shock, Geoff. Although Uncle Noel will be indignant, this diary can't be read by anyone else. I must destroy it.'

'Well, that's up to you. Don't worry. I'll tackle Noel, if you'd like me to.' And then as she was silent: 'Do you want to tell me about it?'

'You're the only person I shall tell. I can't say I *want* to tell even you . . .'

'Then keep it to yourself, sweet. I'm not particularly interested in the secret life of a man I barely knew, who is now dead.'

'But I must tell you. It's your right to know.'

'How can it be my right?'

'It is, because it's about me, as well as – others. I'll have to make a plunge for it, or I'll never get the words out. This diary was written during the year I was born, and he – he

81

says here that my mother and he were lovers, and that I am his child.'

'Good lord!' It took Geoffrey a minute to digest this information, and then he said: 'Are you sure you're not making a mistake? It's general knowledge that Quentin had an idealistic, perhaps a romantic, affection for your mother, and as his sister-in-law, she was pretty close to him, but you could have misread what he wrote.'

'I haven't. You can read it for yourself.'

'You'd rather I didn't, wouldn't you?' Geoffrey said gently.

'Well – yes . . . I'd like to burn it; tear it to pieces. Not that the diary is all about my mother and how he loved her . . . for several months there's only a line now and again when at odd times they were together. They were very careful. He was fond of my father and so was she; they tried not to hurt him, but they seem to have loved overwhelmingly. In the spring of that year my mother knew she was pregnant, and she seems to have had no doubt that Quentin was responsible. They couldn't help being happy about it, because she wanted a child, but after some uncertainty they decided not to tell her husband. He had been away at the time I was conceived, but – but he was far from suspecting, and was so devoted to my mother, they were sure they could pull it off . . . Oh, Geoff, it all became rather furtive and contrived . . . this love they thought so great . . . I suppose all liaisons are the same.'

'Probably.'

'They planned to juggle with the dates. Quentin says it wouldn't have been difficult, as it's well-known that a first baby is sometimes born later than it should be . . . but as it turned out, there was no need for all that elaborate deceit. He describes what torture he went through, knowing that his brother was not only my mother's husband, but her lover. Geoff, I can't think how she could . . . oh, I do want to be understanding, not to condemn her. But to let them both make love to her . . .'

'She had no choice, unless she intended to break with her husband,' Geoffrey said.

82

'But he thought her an angel. He loved her so much that it was years after her death before he re-married; and Quentin, who really knew her, seems also to have thought her an angel. But, as I say, they needn't have worried about discovery, because just about the time I was due to be born, my mother had a slight fall, and everyone, doctor included, imagined that brought me into the world sooner than I was expected. And then only a week later, she died. It was dreadful to read that part of the diary – Quentin was heartbroken.'

Geoffrey sat down beside her on the day-bed, and wrapped his arms around her. 'My poor darling, what a hideous afternoon you have had.'

Clare said sombrely, 'You must feel as though you've married a stranger.'

'What nonsense !'

'I shall never tell Father,' said Clare. 'I mean the one I've always had – though it might make it better for Margery.'

'I doubt it. Of course you won't tell him. Instead of thinking more of Margery, it might make him distrust women. As for you, you won't be able to forget what you've discovered, but you can learn to accept it.'

'But I loved the thought of my mother – as perfect.'

Geoffrey said firmly, 'From all accounts she was a sweet and lovable person. She was weak, but few people are other than weak if they fall passionately in love; but in spite of that, there must have been much of the angel in her since both brothers loved her so devotedly.'

'Why didn't Quentin burn the diary?' Clare lamented. 'Why did he keep it all those years?'

'He probably intended to destroy it. If he had had a long illness, then he would.'

'I wish he had. When I next meet Father . . . I'm so afraid he'll notice the difference in me . . . in my manner.'

'You won't be seeing him again for some months,' Geoffrey soothed.

'That's really a relief. No wonder I adored Quentin, and yet I often felt guilty because he mattered the most to me. I was astounded when I knew he had left me nearly everything

83

he had – but now I see it was natural.'

'Quite natural.'

Geoffrey looked down into her troubled face, and was distressed for her. To him in a personal sense the story mattered nothing. But Clare was suffering hurt and disillusion, and a shattering sense of being different from the person she had believed herself to be.

'If you had known before you married me, would it have made any difference?' she asked.

'You sweet fool! If your parents had been criminals I would still have wanted you.'

With a long, deep sigh, she turned to him, and suddenly remembering the incident of the night before, Geoffrey was ashamed. If Angela had not awakened and he had not heard her moving about and her footsteps on the stairs, there was little doubt that he would have taken Joan. Not only desire, but anger with Clare would have overcome his scruples.

He was in no mood to make excuses for himself. Joan's wantonness should have been repellent, and as for Clare's coldness, he was to blame, had been to blame from the beginning. He had loved her with an iron selfishness, but now his heart or soul had suffered a change, and he found that he desired her happiness before his own. He wanted children no more than he had ever wanted them. His neurosis, or complex, was as strong as it had ever been, but against this, his love for Clare was fighting, though even now it was not an entirely selfless one, for if he gave in to her, he would win her completely, as it seemed he could not win while he deliberately denied her the children she desired.

Only a short while ago he had been determined to break her down. Now he no longer wanted to, but it occurred to him that his willingness to give way to her would stamp out, before it had time to take root in her mind, any suspicion that the irregularity of her birth was of importance to him.

He had been holding her gently in his arms, with his cheek resting on her bright hair, and for Clare the sense of shock and strain was broken. Warmth stole back into her chilled body, and tears relieved the weight which pressed upon her heart.

84

'I'll burn the diary and make up some story which will satisfy old Noel,' Geoffrey said. 'Where is the thing?'

Clare produced the book from beneath the cushions of the day-bed, and Geoffrey took it, went over to the empty fireplace, and while she watched him, he tore out the pages in the book, struck a match and set fire to them. When they blazed up, he added the leather cover to the flames. 'Feel better?' he asked, as he returned to her.

'Much.'

But Geoffrey noticed with some anxiety that there were dark bruises of exhaustion and grief beneath her eyes. Her look of radiant health was rarely dimmed, but it was dimmed now.

'Nobody else will ever know about this,' he said, 'and later on it won't seem so important to you. Now, as you're completely tired out, you had better not go downstairs again today. I'll tell them you have a headache and look after you myself. Bed is what you need and a meal on a tray. No one will come near you. I'll see to it all.'

His thought was that he could not endure Joan to approach her. Something would have to be done about her, and speedily. Meanwhile, Clare needed him, and he could be tender when necessary, though he was more often demanding. Bending over her, he started to unfasten her dress, which buttoned from collar to hem, and when she sobbingly resisted him, he said: 'It's all right . . . I'm not going to make love to you, so stop wriggling. It's as well for me to get in some practice as a nurserymaid, for one day in an emergency I may have to try my hand at undressing a weeping infant instead of a weeping wife.'

He heard her catch her breath. 'Geoff!' she murmured incredulously.

'Is it enough to say I've been wrong, or must I get down on my knees to you?'

'Do you — do you mean it?'

'Well, we can't go on like this. I want a happy wife, but perhaps I've no right to it, unless I give you what you want, a nursery full of brats.'

'It'll be no good, if you hate it,' she faltered.

85

'It may turn out better than I anticipated, and at least I shan't see you becoming more and more of an icicle with every day that passes.' And then as she began to sob, he said grimly: 'Now what's the matter?'

'I want you to be happy too,' she said.

'The chances are I shall be happy if I see you content. Stand up, I can't get your arm out of this sleeve.'

She rose obediently, and Geoffrey smiled, because with the tears running down her cheeks, she looked like a chided child, as she stood there before him. He took off her dress and pulled her to him. 'You're so lovely,' he muttered. 'I shall hate to see you spoilt.'

'It may not happen,' she said brokenly. 'You almost make me hope it won't. I shall always love you best.'

'Quite sure of that?'

'Oh Geoff, of course I'm sure, but how can I help wanting to have babies? Most women do – it's the way they're made. I do so want to give you a son.'

For the first time, as he held her close to him, his heart was stirred by this thought. It was a primitive reaction which he despised, and yet could not deny.

'I adore you,' he said gently.

'I know you do – now,' she murmured. 'I was never sure before. I've been afraid . . .'

'Not that I should stop loving you, surely?'

'No, I was afraid I might stop loving you. I was beginning to hate it so . . . To have you admiring my body, which seemed such a useless, barren body. All the ways of love tired and bored me. It was as though I was unreal, a kind of puppet . . . I've tried to tell you this before.'

'And I wouldn't listen to you.'

'You didn't want to listen, or to believe it was important, but you do now, don't you?'

'Yes, I do now.'

'I knew I was – unsatisfactory,' she said painfully, 'though you would never agree; not until the other night, when you left me in anger. That hurt and humiliated me, but now I'm glad you did, for it was then you started to realize that our kind of love-making is futile.'

'Naturally it's futile to make love to a frigid woman.'

'But I'm not that, Geoff.'

'Are you sure?'

'Was I when we first married?'

'You've changed since those days, when you accepted me unquestioningly. For months, though you've not rejected me openly, you've rejected me in your heart and soul.'

'It was as though I was your mistress, not your wife.'

'That's been the accusation of many a cold woman. Is it a crime if you're a mixture of both to me?'

'No. I want to be everything to you.'

'For biological reasons, I suppose?'

'Geoff, you've got to understand . . . it's the same with me, as with you . . . a mixture of loving; thinking of you as my husband as well as my lover . . . adoring you if you gave me children.'

He unkindly said, 'There's a chance you may not be a fruitful vine.'

'Of course, but as long as it's not deliberate I can bear it, though I should grieve and be disappointed.'

He softened to her. 'Don't worry. There's little doubt you'll have your nursery of babies. I shall have to work hard to keep them; for make no mistake about that, our family will be my financial responsibility, not yours.'

'I want them to be,' she said softly. 'You'll love them all the better for it.'

'It seems only the other day I first had you in my arms. How sweet you were on our wedding night. Do you remember?'

'I was scared. I didn't know what to expect – but you . . . you were a wonderful lover, Geoff . . . oh, darling . . .!'

'Shall I take you off on a second honeymoon?' he suggested. 'This week-end? Away from all these old people who make constant demands on you? Away from this house, where you've not been too happy of late?'

Clare gazed at him with fascinated eyes. 'It would be lovely – but how can we? There's Angela. She's our guest. There's your music too.'

'I can leave my music for a week-end. Actually it might

be as well. What I've done is good, but it needs revision with a clear mind, and a short break might help. As for Angela, she's happy enough with the rest of them and can spare us a few days. It's a long time since we've been in London together, and we might be able to get the same suite of rooms at that hotel.'

'The Venice? I loved it there.'

'I'll ring up when I've got you into bed and see if we can reserve a suite from tomorrow. Tonight you shall rest undisturbed. I'll sleep in the dressing-room.'

'But, Geoff – that isn't necessary.'

'I think it is,' he said inflexibly. 'Your feeling is that you've never been properly my wife, so we'll make a fresh start, but not here, and not tonight. In London we can be completely on our own for a few days, though I suppose we shall have to return for Nichol's party, since he's making it seem so important.'

She protested and he laughed. It was a new experience to sense her rebellion, to know that for the first time it was she who wanted him.

'What you need is a sedative,' he said firmly.

'I don't . . . I feel quite well and calm, and I won't be put to bed as though I'm a silly child.'

'You are a silly child. Turn round – this thing unhooks at the back, doesn't it?'

'Please, Geoff . . .'

'Don't make a fuss.'

'It's ridiculous to treat me like this. I shall be more unhappy, if I have to stay here alone – in bed, as though I'm ill, when I'm not.'

'You'll do as you're told,' he said with sudden harshness. 'For my own reasons I want you to stay up here, and out of the way until I can carry you off tomorrow. It's not much to ask you.'

Clare said dazedly, 'I don't understand . . . is there something I'm not meant to understand?'

'Perhaps, but can't you trust me?'

'Yes, I suppose so,' she agreed reluctantly, but the tears had started again.

'Didn't I tell you that you were overwrought? You're not usually a crying woman.'

'So much has happened today – too much,' she said grievously.

'Exactly, and if I can help it, nothing more will happen until I can get you away from here.'

'But do you still love me, Geoff?'

'Very much. Here, let me dry your eyes.'

He took his handkerchief and dabbed at her face, and suddenly she clung to him not with childish dependence but with passion and intensity. Geoff was so surprised that he abruptly sat down on the day-bed, and Clare with a sigh of relief, curled into his arms and put her mouth to his.

'Now it's you who are cold to me,' she said accusingly.

'That must be a new experience for you. Is it a pleasant one?'

'No. Don't be hateful.'

'Darling!'

It was impossible to wholly resist her, and he caressed her gently as he said, 'I know what's best for you. Calm down and give me my own way for once.'

'You've always had your own way,' she said resentfully.

'That's how it should be.' This was said too seriously to please her.

'Don't you want me any more?'

'You know the answer to that, or if not, I'll give you one when we're in London together.'

'We shall have to come back.'

But not until Joan had gone, he thought resolutely, and he would no longer be reminded of her. In effect he would be setting his house in order, though it would undoubtedly run less smoothly without Joan's organizing ability.

Later in the evening, when Clare, having had a meal in bed, followed by two aspirins, was asleep, Geoffrey went to the garden-room and rang the bell. Joan appeared in answer to it, and he said, 'Shut the door. I want to talk to you.'

In her dark dress, with a lace and muslin apron tied around her waist, Joan looked very different from the bacchante of the night before, and she faced him composedly. She said, 'I

89

thought you might.'

It was difficult to say what must be said, but Geoffrey forced himself to speak bluntly. 'I'm sorry, Joan, but you'll have to leave.'

'Leave?' She stared at him in amazement. 'But why? What have I done?'

'We might both have acted regrettably last night, if we hadn't been interrupted,' Geoffrey said, hating himself for the smug words, but unable to find others.

'But Miss Rose suspected nothing.'

'I'm not concerned with Miss Rose. This is between ourselves. I blame myself as much as you . . .'

'You don't!' Joan's voice was scornful. 'Why should you? You wouldn't have thought of making love to me if I hadn't acted the way I did. But I told you it wouldn't make any difference; that nobody would ever know, that I'd behave – in public – as I've always behaved.'

Geoffrey sighed. He said, 'You make me feel a shocking prig. I won't talk about morals or self-respect, but only say that if you and I had to live under the same roof the whole set-up would be too uncomfortable. I'm taking Mrs Deering to London this week-end, and while we're away, you must pack up and leave. Write to her or send her a message, make what excuse you like, but don't be here when we return.'

'Suppose I refuse,' Joan said, her voice shaking. 'Suppose I say I'll only take my notice from her.'

'Then I shall have to tell her,' Geoffrey said.

'You couldn't!'

'There'd be nothing else for it. I'd hate it naturally. It would be a shock to her, but she would understand, I think – or at least she would understand my behaviour . . . not yours perhaps, not so easily.'

'She's fond of me,' Joan said, 'and I'm fond of her. I never meant her any harm. I wouldn't have taken from her anything she'd have missed.'

Geoffrey shook his head. 'It's no good, Joan. I'm really sorry. You were with us through all our hard times, and you've been of great value to us . . .'

'But you wanted me. Last night you wanted me as much as

90

I wanted you,' Joan pleaded. 'Don't you like me?'

'I've never liked you. My wife has, and does – but time and again I'd have preferred to do without you. I admit you made us comfortable, saved us money, all that and more . . . but I'd rather have seen my wife muddle through on her own. Now she'll have to.'

'It'll be a muddle all right,' Joan said grimly. 'She's been living in a dream for years – that's the sort she is. She's depended on me.'

'Too much,' Geoffrey agreed.

As Joan was silent, he went to his desk and took out his cheque-book. 'I'll pay you three months' wages,' he said, 'and of course you'll get a reference, if you want one.'

The girl laughed outright. She said, 'It's easy to see you're new to this kind of game. A nice fool you'd be to write me a cheque. I'd only have to show it to her, and she'd know you sent me off, and that there was some secret reason for it. I don't want your money anyway. Keep it. I've saved, and I could get higher wages anywhere. I've only to drop Mrs Moore a line at Le Touquet and she'll jump at having me. Yes, even if you do tell a tale about me being no better than I should be.'

Geoffrey, baffled, could well believe it, and Joan went on lashing herself to anger.

'She'd never believe you; me who's been in the family for all these years and nobody to say a word against me. Oh, I'll go all right, and though you're looking a fool this minute, it's me who's really the fool, for I might have known how it would be. I'll leave a message to say I was called away to look after an old aunt, who's ill. Mrs Deering knows I have one – my mother's elder sister she is, and alone in the world. But I despise the way you've tackled this. If you didn't like me, you should have got rid of me long ago, and if that's a lie, and you're afraid of me, why can't you say so?'

'Too cowardly, I suppose,' Geoffrey said.

Unexpectedly, she softened. 'Well, I dare say most men would be. Though it was a mean thing to say you never liked me.'

'Perhaps it was. What I really meant was that I've often

felt you had too much influence, were too dominating, and that we both depended on you too much.'

'I've done no more than any servant would do, who was capable and had been with you a long time. Couldn't you forget about last night, if I promise I shan't let it happen again?'

'I'm sorry . . .'

Joan sighed and then she shrugged. 'Very well, have it your own way, but I don't like leaving her and that's a fact. I mind it more than not having you make love to me. I shan't forget you though, and you won't forget me . . . there will be times when you'll think of me and wonder what it would have been like, to have me as a lover.'

For an instant her gaze rested on him, half mocking, half regretful, and then she shrugged again, opened the door and went out.

Geoffrey's state of mind was much as Clare's had been earlier in the evening. Too much had happened in the space of a few hours.

6

'You say you've heard nothing about the contents of the book in the secret drawer, but you must have some idea of the reaction it caused,' Nichol said.

'The only reaction is that Clare has kept to her room ever since, and that Geoffrey is taking her to London for the weekend. He told Noel Moore that the diary was too private and personal in spots to be shown to anyone, and that on his advice Clare had burnt it. The old man was peeved, but Geoffrey was quite unconcerned.'

Angela also seemed unconcerned, as she walked along the sands by Nichol's side. There was silent amusement in her eyes as she added, 'You can't blame me if things are not turning out just as you expected. I've followed your instructions.'

'I've not blamed you as yet. Have you any idea why Deering is taking Clare away this week-end?'

'Not a ghost of a one, but surely you, with your out-of-this-world divination, should be able to delve into both their minds.'

'What I can do, or not, is no concern of yours,' Nichol said, 'and why, may I ask, are you so much more cheerful today — and unafraid?'

'Perhaps because I've a notion that I've less cause to fear than I supposed,' Angela said slowly. 'I admit you have power, but . . .'

'Well?' he interjected.

'Why should I tell you the thoughts I have, the conjectures I've made . . . you who are a mind reader?'

'You need not,' he said coldly.

There was silence as they walked along, side by side. Angela was deep in her thoughts which she realized had been confused for days, and were only now starting to achieve coherence. The best thing she could do, she told herself, would be to write down the conclusions to which she was hazily groping her way. This was a habit of hers. Tersely stated on paper, facts had a way of becoming comfortingly lucid.

'You will investigate the matter of the pearls,' Nichol said, and the words were couched not as a query or suggestion, but as a command.

'Yes — at my first opportunity. Noel Moore did take them, I suppose? Oh, very well,' as this was met with blank silence, 'I realize that you probably know already, and it's only part of what you call my training that I have to find out. The thing is, that whatever I do find out or bring about doesn't seem to make the trouble for these people that it evidently should make. For instance, I discovered Geoffrey and that girl together, and it confounded neither of them.'

'It will confound Clare when you tell her,' Nichol said grimly, 'and you will do that before they leave for London tonight. Your information may affect the tempo of their short holiday.'

'I dare say it will,' Angela agreed.

But not, she thought privately, in the way Nichol supposed. With all his dark power – and although she now had her comforting doubts, she did not underrate them – he appeared to have little understanding of the way in which a woman's mind worked.

'There's no doubt, I suppose,' Nichol said, 'that they will return in time for the party?'

'None whatever, I imagine, but if they thought of sidetracking it, you would find means of bringing them back.'

'I should,' Nichol said. 'Poor girl – it's a pity . . .'

He broke off and Angela said curiously, 'You actually like her. I do believe she's the chink in your armour, if there is one. You half-regret making her unhappy. Although you connect her with Ceres, it's much more likely she represents Proserpina to you. But you'll never half-win her as Proserpina was half-won. She belongs to the world of light, and not only for six months in the year.'

He stopped still in his walk to look at her, but Angela turned her head aside – she wouldn't gaze into those bright, dark, curiously blank eyes and thus again be caught up in a mesh of fear.

'It's extremely unwise to take that tone with me,' Nichol said quietly.

'Yes, it probably is. Have you finished with me for now? If I'm to talk to Clare before Geoffrey takes her off this afternoon, I haven't too much time.'

'That's true – you can go. But let me warn you, if you have any frivolous ideas about evading the issue . . .'

'Whatever else they are, my ideas are certainly not frivolous. I've set foot in a world I should have shunned at all costs, and I'll have to pay the penalty, and I feel as strongly as I did in the beginning, that I'm compelled to carry out your instructions.'

He watched her frowningly as she sped away from him along the sands; watched her climb the cliff pathway to 'Welcomes'. She was his creature – there was no escape for her, and that she knew – but what she said was disturbing. Her suspicion, for one thing, of his secret weakness. The pitiless had no weak-

ness. If her random suspicion became more than a suspicion
. . . In the curious eyes there was a flicker of apprehension.

*

Clare was packing her case for the week-end, a task which
normally would have been left to Joan, but Joan today was
elusive. Of course there was always extra work at the week-
end, but it did not as a rule take her the entire morning to
do the shopping in the village.

Thankful that her best evening dress was of white lace
which was easy to pack, Clare laid it out on the carpet, and
started to fold the wide skirt. She was carefully lifting it into
her case, when Angela knocked on the door and came in.

'Are you better?' she asked. 'Geoff said you had such
a bad headache that you weren't to be bothered by anyone.'

'It has gone,' Clare said. 'Do you mind being left alone
for the week-end? Geoff thinks I need to get away from
everyone for a few days.'

Angela sat down on the arm of a chair and said, 'Go on
packing, while I talk to you. What I have to say may be
disturbing, though I hope you won't let it be – you needn't.'

'What is it?'

'It seems best to tell you. The night before last I fell
asleep while Geoffrey was practising in the garden-room. I
think I still heard the music in my sleep. When I woke up,
it had stopped, and I was bewildered and scared. I couldn't
stay in my room alone, and I thought I'd see if Geoff was
still in the garden-room – I was in a nervous state, I suppose.
Well, he *was* there, and Joan was with him, in her dressing-
gown. She had heard him playing, she said, and she came
across to the house to make tea for him. But I'm sure her
real object was to make love.'

'Angela, that's an extraordinary thing to say,' Clare protested.

'My dear, she's that sort of girl; one of those girls who
look very proper and reserved, and are really the reverse.
You're such an innocent you wouldn't recognize the type,
but I've met it before. Geoffrey's very attractive, and I

95

wanting to do Joan a bad turn, but I'm very fond of you, that's why I'm telling you. Do get rid of her.'

Clare continued to pack. She tucked a pair of soft bedroom slippers into the corner of the case, went to the dressing-table for her brushes and a pot of face-cream.

'I've known Joan all my life,' she said.

'I doubt if you've ever known her. Geoff must have been taken by surprise, but those quiet, subtle girls are dangerous, and can be attractive. Joan did look attractive, though she'd bundled up her hair, which I'm convinced was hanging loose until a moment before I walked in on them. Why on earth should she have got out of her bed to make tea for Geoff? Or if she did, why not have dressed properly?'

'It's a hateful thing to believe of anyone,' said Clare. 'And how can I get rid of Joan just because of a vague suspicion — perhaps not even that?'

Angela shrugged. 'Well, it's up to you, but if I had a husband, however devoted, I wouldn't trust him with her. You're beautiful in your own way, but a girl such as that has something more than beauty; an animal magnetism, because she *is* an animal.'

'Oh, don't!'

'A decent man wants more, of course,' Angela went on remorselessly, 'and Geoff is decent, but they all have their weak moments.'

For a moment the two girls looked at one another in silence, and then Angela said, 'I expect you think I'm cruel to have told you all this, just as you're starting off on a holiday with Geoff. I wish now I hadn't. I don't want to upset anyone here, and you I love . . .'

'I believe you do,' Clare said with some astonishment.

'You'll be all the wiser and stronger for knowing what you're up against. Don't look so worried. This is not a happy house just now, you'll be glad to get away, and when you return — well, I can only see a little way ahead, but I think you'll be too strong and too secure for anyone to frighten you.'

'Angela — sometimes you're so strange, I only half understand you.'

Angela, at the door and on the verge of departing, smiled over her shoulder.

'You understand enough. For pity's sake, you fool, forget about everything, except Geoff.'

Clare gazed at the closed door for a few moments, then she swiftly strapped the suitcase, and went to the wardrobe for her coat and hat. She put them on before a mirror, and perhaps for the first time in her life was grateful for her beauty.

Incidents which had puzzled her were now explained. Joan was explained – her reticences and her moods – her exaggerated attentiveness to Geoffrey. Although Clare had attempted to defend Joan, she had little doubt that Angela's suspicions were justified, for it was clear that during the last day Geoffrey had deliberately kept Joan at a distance from her.

Clare shivered slightly. How patient Joan had been, and how closely she must have observed Geoffrey, to realize at last that he was on the verge of breaking. The situation which had developed was largely her own fault. Her coldness had been deliberate and stubborn. It was not her fault that their union had been imperfect, but she could have shown more tenderness and understanding. If she had, Geoffrey would have given way long ago. But her frozen passivity had hardened his heart. As for Joan, it was doubtful, thought Clare, if she would ever understand her, but something of affection still lingered, though she might never see her again.

Angela had urged her to get rid of Joan, but that was unnecessary, for Clare was sure Geoffrey had already made his plans. It would be no surprise to her on their return from London to find that Joan had gone. Perhaps she ought to be grateful to her, for it was after the scene with Joan that Geoffrey had changed and softened; though this might have been partly caused by the discovery of Clare's birth secret.

A love child!

The ironical description flashed across her mind, but not now with any sense of shame, for she had indeed been conceived in love, was the fruit of no casual liaison but a great if unlawful passion. How could anyone thus born be lethargic, unresponsive, insensitive? Yet it seemed to her that she had

97

been all of these things.

Her spirit had needed some quickening touch; she had been only half-alive until Geoffrey had changed to her. Now she was aware of a reviving vitality, and confidence. All these years, Joan had held the household reins in her capable hands, but henceforth Clare would depend on herself, would learn to housekeep, learn to be a more satisfactory wife, and perhaps should Fate be kind . . .

Resolutely she pushed the thought away from her. She would not let herself hope too much; she would make Geoffrey realize that he could be enough for her, if it was their destiny to be childless. In that case she wouldn't fret or repine. Nichol, strange creature that he was, persistently likened her to the Earth-Mother, but Demeter had been ruthless, willing to destroy all the fruitful world when her own child was lured into darkness.

There was an analogy in this somewhere, thought Clare, trying to puzzle it out. It had been a cruel revenge on a world which had not been responsible for her deprivation. Had she in a small way followed Demeter's example? Had she been wilfully negative, dreaming her days away, making little effort to cope with reality?

She heard Geoffrey come in, and turned towards him.

'Ready?' he asked.

She nodded, and slipped her hand into his.

*

'You promised to show me your collection of jade,' Angela said. 'Wouldn't this be a good opportunity?'

At Becky's invitation, Angela and Noel and Phillis were having tea in the theatre wing. It was Sunday afternoon and without the presence of their host and hostess, the old people preferred their own quarters, and Becky had decided on a tea-party, ignoring the fact that this meant extra work for Marty, who was usually permitted to rest in her room on a Sunday afternoon.

In Becky's big room, tables had been set out, and she had dug into her constantly accumulating stores, and had produced tins of petits-fours, rich plum cake, *pâté de foie gras* and preserved fruit. With Sunday papers strewn around, and

98

bottles of liqueurs of fantastic shape and brilliant colouring, the scene was one of rich disorder, over which Becky presided with autocracy.

'That's the third cherry brandy, Phillis, and it'll be the last,' she said. 'I don't grudge it to you, heaven knows, but I'll not be responsible for starting you on a jag.'

'Really, Becky, what things you say!' Phillis expostulated. 'I never take a little drinkie except for my nerves.'

'You can make your nerves an excuse when you go to Nichol's party next Tuesday. But stick to port, that's your tipple. Gin or brandy excites you too much.'

Phillis shuddered and protested that she dreaded the thought of entering that dreadful cottage, but felt it would be her duty, as the poor young man was brave enough to live there and probably needed to keep up his morale by having visitors.

It was under cover of this bickering that Angela, sitting near to Noel, bent nearer to him, and suggested that he might care to exhibit his collection of jade. 'Actually, I possess a tiny piece which you might like to have,' she said. 'It's a miniature paper-knife.'

'My dear child, that's more than sweet of you, but I couldn't possibly accept it,' Noel said.

'Oh, nonsense! It's only a trifle, and I don't care about it. If we could slip away now, I'd fetch it and bring it along to your room.'

'Well, really . . . I don't know what to say.'

'Let's go,' said Angela, a laughing light in her eyes.

Noel was flattered and also greedily pleased. He rose and so did Angela, but not without attracting Becky's attention.

'Oh, very well,' she agreed grudgingly, when Angela explained, 'but don't be all night up there, examining Noel's treasures. I thought we might have a game of cards as there's nothing else to do. The more players the merrier. Marty, what about roping in Joan? She's not out today, is she?'

Marty said she thought Joan was in her room, resting, whereupon Becky said the girl was probably bored to tears and would be delighted to be invited.

'I loathe cards, and shall go for a walk rather than be

forced to play,' Angela said, when she and Noel had escaped from the room. 'How about you?'

'Well, it's not my idea of an enjoyable game, to play for pennies,' Noel said, 'but I often do, to divert the old dear. However, we shall be allowed an hour's grace, I dare say.'

'Wait while I fetch the paper-knife,' Angela said.

'I'll go ahead and light up, but I warn you my room is in a litter – papers almost knee-deep. Inevitable, since I only have one room as sitting-room and bedroom.'

Angela gave him a full ten minutes, which he employed in fussily putting his room to rights, though with the exception of his desk in one corner, which was, as always, piled high with books and papers, it was tidy enough.

'How nice you have made it look,' Angela said with genuine approval when she knocked and was admitted. 'Is all this delightful furniture your own?'

'Most of it. I've bought odd pieces from time to time, but the functional stuff was here when I first decided to make my home with dear old Quentin.'

Angela observed the valuable Persian rug which covered the divan bed, the one or two good pictures, the Queen Anne chairs. These certainly represented money, and it was problematical how Noel, who possessed only a tiny income, had managed to acquire them.

Perhaps guessing her thoughts, he said, 'I didn't noise it abroad, but dear old Quentin was generous to me, and when I saw a piece I coveted, he often insisted on paying for it. He was of the opinion that poor Isabel had treated me far from well. I gave up my life to her for years, and in return, when she died, I received less than a servant's pension.'

Angela murmured commiseratingly, and Noel said gallantly, 'What charm you lend to my poor abode. It's not often I have the opportunity to entertain youth and beauty. Now, if you will sit in that high-backed chair, I will draw it up to my cabinet. As you see, I can switch on lights in the cabinet above each shelf, so that the collection can be seen to advantage. I have some pretty pieces, though as Becky rightly told you, nothing of extreme value . . .'

'First let me give you my little contribution,' Angela said.

'Yes – please, I really want you to have it. The Maharajah gave it to me because I happened to fancy it, and he taught me quite a lot about jade, which was one of his subjects. He was a connoisseur.'

'I remember hearing so, or reading about it, at the time of your marriage to him,' Noel said, and exclaimed with pleasure when Angela proffered a piece of jade which, as she had said, was a small piece, though of good colour and intricately carved.

Noel's cabinet was well stocked, and Angela admired several pieces which were more showy than beautiful. At first she sat in the high-backed chair, and examined specimens which Noel took from the cabinet and put into her hands, but presently she rose and said, 'May I explore? That's a charming little piece in the background, so is the mirror with the jade frame.'

As she slid her hand into the cabinet, Noel made an involuntary movement as though to check her, but she appeared not to notice, and carefully drew out the figure of a small Chinese boy, trundling a barrow, and the little mirror which was framed in white jade and heavily wreathed with pale green grapes. There was fruit also in the barrow; smooth globes in various colours representing oranges and apples and melons.

'But these are not jade, surely?' Angela said.

'No. They're semi-precious stones,' Noel replied. 'Onyx and rose quartz and moonstones.'

He watched Angela uneasily, as she took the two pieces and examined them more closely beneath the central light. 'Rather odd to introduce them into jade carvings,' she said innocently. 'They must have been added later. Why yes, they've been fixed with glue or something of the kind. How very odd.'

'It's not a good piece, I fear,' Noel said. 'I picked it up in a junk shop for next to nothing.'

'Not part of your wife's collection, then?'

'Oh no, I only bought it a year or so ago.'

'And the mirror too? Why, these grapes are all of different sizes, beautifully graduated, but not one of them identical.

Some of them are quite loose – see! Good gracious, you could easily lose them.'

Before Noel could stop her, or indeed grasp her intention, she had taken up the jade paper-knife, and had carefully inserted the stiletto-like point beneath one of the smaller grapes, which in an instant was dislodged and fell into her hand.

'Take care!' Noel cried sharply.

Ignoring him, Angela turned the green bead over on her palm. She lightly scraped the point of the knife across it, just where a minute spot of some fixative had caused it to adhere to the frame. She heard Noel's stifled exclamation, realized that he had slumped down into the chair where she had been sitting and turned to look at him.

'Quite a neat camouflage,' she said, 'but it wouldn't deceive an expert. It's lucky for you that nobody ever suggested a thorough examination of your collection.'

Noel returned her gaze with haggard eyes. He said, 'You meant to trap me.'

'Yes. I wanted to find out for myself.'

'But why? What business is it of yours? Or – did her family suggest this to you, offer you a reward if you discovered . . .?'

'That you had taken the pearls, your wife's fabulously valuable necklace?'

'It should have been mine. All she possessed should have been mine. Time and again when I threatened to leave her, she told me she would reward me if I stayed. And then when she died, I knew she'd cheated me, for the only will she'd ever made was soon after we were married, and all she had, with the exception of my miserly trust fund, was left to her family. It was then I remembered the pearls. Only a few months before her death she'd had a replica made, meaning to put the real pearls in a safe deposit, but she delayed doing that, and I knew where to find them. It seemed safe enough, as nobody but myself knew of the existence of the artificial pearls, and it wasn't suspected until I'd got clean away to England, having first broken up the pearls and sewn them into the lining of coats and hats and shoes. Then, though I knew her people suspected me, they had no proof – and how or when they got in touch with you – or why you, wealthy as you are, let yourself be bribed – I don't know.'

'I've not been bribed,' said Angela. 'I know nothing about your wife's people, but when I heard the story, I was sure . . .'

'You mean you trapped me out of curiosity?'

'Call it that.'

Noel's face had become the colour of parchment, his mouth was working loosely, his eyes pleaded with her. He said, 'What do you mean to do about it?'

'I'm not sure. Have you sold any of the pearls?'

'Two of them – the largest . . . to a dealer I know. We were boys at school together, but he was always a wrong 'un – likeable enough, though. I kept up with him through the years and he's acted fairly by me.' And then as Angela was silent, he repeated : 'What do you mean to do about it?'

'It all depends – not on me primarily,' she said vaguely.

'Keep a close mouth, and I'll give you half of them,' Noel said agitatedly.

'I don't want them. I'm not interested in the pearls – though it'll be interesting to discover . . .'

'To discover what?' demanded Noel, unable to follow her disjointed thoughts.

'Never mind.' Angela picked up the mirror, and then the Chinese figure with the barrel of camouflaged fruit, and handed them to him. 'Put these back in safety,' she said.

Noel was shaking pitiably as he obeyed her. He did not trust her and his fear was as great as his hatred of her. Angela smiled as she said, 'Yes, of course you'd like to strangle me, but you can't do it here and now. I should put up a fight, and even if you succeeded, you'd be hanged for it. But as a fact, you're in no danger from me. I shan't expose you – it wouldn't amuse me, and it would be distressing for Clare. Your fate doesn't lie in my hands.'

'In whose then?'

'That remains to be seen. Close the cabinet, and then we'd better go back to the others and take part in the card games. I shan't go for a walk, after all.'

'For heaven's sake!' Noel cried, 'How can I play childish

103

games with this on my mind? Tell Becky I'm not feeling well — and that I have to rest.'

'Very well,' Angela said mockingly and left him.

Noel sat huddled in his chair, his hands covering his face. Now and again he uttered a shuddering groan. Exposure would mean ruin, for his wife's family, who had always disliked him, would certainly not spare him. But he judged that it was already too late to wreak vengeance on Angela. She was shrewd and careful, he thought, and she would probably take good care to leave some message or letter, which if an ill-fate befell her, would be the ruination of him.

He was so sunk in despair that he did not hear the gentle knock on the door until it was repeated, and then he started up with a gasp of terror as Joan came in.

'Why, Mr Noel, whatever is the matter?' she cried, and ran to him, urging him back into his chair. 'I saw Miss Rose come down the stairs, and I thought you'd be alone, and you're the one person I felt I had to see before I left. I wouldn't like to go without saying goodbye.'

'Saying goodbye?' Noel repeated dazedly. 'Where are you going then?'

'I don't know as yet, not for sure. To London first, I expect. But don't you worry about me now, Mr Noel. You're looking really ill. A spot of brandy is what you need, and if you'll wait, I'll get some from Miss Redcliffe.'

'You needn't. There's a bottle in the cupboard.'

Joan brought the bottle and a glass and poured him a liberal measure, saying it would be all the better if he took it straight. She pulled the electric fire nearer to him, and took a cushion from the divan to put behind his head.

'You're a good girl, Joan.' Noel patted her hand. 'You've always been a kind, considerate girl to me, besides being a pretty one. Come, sit down here near me, and tell me what you meant by saying you were going away. That's nonsense; you can't be spared.'

'Oh yes, I can; they'll be better off without me, and apart from that, I'm sick to death of it here. I'm off first thing tomorrow, before he or she come back, and then there won't be any fuss from either of them, trying to make me change my mind.'

'Joan – for the lord's sake, stop this nonsense! If they can do without you, I can't. You know how much I depend on you; how fond I am of you. Why, if I were a younger man, I . . .' He broke off and Joan waited expectantly. 'If I were even ten years younger, I should have been in love with you by now,' Noel finished.

'I wouldn't say a man's age has anything to do with falling in love.' Joan's gaze rested on him speculatively. 'And you're not as old as that, Mr Noel. You're still a fine figure of a man.'

He shook his head in dolorous self-pity. 'I'm old and tired – too tired to cope, and very lonely.'

'It's not much of a life for you here, and that's a fact,' Joan agreed, 'cooped up with two old women, and nobody taking any interest in you or your work. I've often wondered why you didn't marry again. Not a woman such as your first, but a young woman who you could be proud of, and who'd take a pleasure in looking after you.'

'No young woman would look at me, Joan.'

'Well, now that's nonsense for if I were your class, Mr Noel, I'd be flattered if you fell in love with me. But as I am not – well, it'd be a kind of insult anyway, if you did.'

'An insult! My dear girl, you know very well that I honour and admire you. I'm shattered at the thought of you leaving, the one real friend I've had ever since dear old Quentin died. There's nothing I wouldn't do to keep you here.'

Joan pulled two cushions from the divan, threw them on the floor at his feet and gracefully disposed herself upon them. As though it were familiar and natural to her, she leaned against his knees, sitting sideways, with her face upturned to him. 'I can't stay here,' she said, 'but then neither need you unless you want to. Why not come with me?'

Noel was speechless with surprise, but he was also fascinated. He looked down on her, young and lithe and as graceful as a cat. Youth, he thought longingly, comely youth, and she was offering it to him – or was she? He seemed to see her

105

with new eyes – her grace, her clear, white skin, her plentiful hair, shining and well brushed.

'What do you mean?' he asked.

Unexpectedly her face crinkled with laughter. She said, 'Mr Noel, I've gone as far as a girl can be expected to go. I've given you a lead. Now it's up to you; but I will say that I'd not be likely to make you ashamed of me. I've a good manner, so people say, and I know how to dress, and I know your ways.'

'Do you mean – *would* you marry me then, Joan?'

'I would if I was asked.'

'My dear girl, I must be nearly forty years older than you.'

'What of it? You're young for your age, and you've got looks and you're a gentleman. There's been many a good marriage with just such a difference in age.'

'Yes, but nearly always the man in such a case has been wealthy. I can't hang you with jewels, or buy you sables. I have a very small income, as you must realize.'

Joan looked at him long and steadily, and then she looked away.

'Not sables or diamonds, but we could have a nice home. I'm a good manager. I promise you I'd see you were comfortable, and I'd be proud of you, and your name too, if you gave it to me. You're not that poor, Mr Noel . . . buying yourself what you fancy from time to time; a miniature or a picture or a piece of old furniture. I'm not asking any questions, but each time you went to London, once or twice a year it's been, you've brought me back a present, and you've had money, which I banked for you myself once, when you had the bronchitis and couldn't get out.'

Noel was startled, but not alarmed. She could not possibly know anything about the pearls, but she was intelligent enough to realize that he must have some secret store of wealth.

'From time to time I've sold certain valuables,' he said with dignity. 'I have also by good fortune invested part of the money they fetched in stocks and shares which have done well. You wouldn't starve if you were my wife, and you wouldn't have to go out to work, but we should have to be careful.'

'There's none better able to be careful than me,' she said, 'and I can see you're a clever one with money – and secret, not letting one of them here suspect. That's something for a girl to respect, a man who can be secret and steadily make his profits and not boast about it. I've saved money myself, out of my wages and presents Mrs Deering gave me . . . we're two of a kind, it seems.'

'I shouldn't wonder.'

His heart warmed to her as it had not warmed to any woman for years. Destiny, he thought, had not yet finished with him, and this evening it was taking a surprising turn. But then nothing had been normally comfortable and dull these last few weeks; not since that half-drowned witch girl had been brought to the house.

But Joan was speaking again, in her calm and reasonable voice, and listening to her, he forgot Angela.

'I'd play fair with you,' she said, 'as you'd play fair with me. I'd not ask you to insure your life for as big a sum as possible, and then one night put sleeping-pills into your hot milk and rum.'

At this horrifying suggestion, delivered with an entire lack of emotion, Noel shuddered and uttered a shocked exclamation, at which Joan laughed softly. She put one of her hands on his knee and pressed it. 'I bet it happens often enough, and there's no proof against the wife, though there might be suspicion – but I wouldn't want you out of the way. I'd be proud if, through my care, you lived to be a hundred; proud that people should see the fine old gentleman you still would be. But you're not old yet – not really old yet . . .'

'Well, I still have a bit of life in me, I hope,' Noel agreed complacently.

How was it that he had never before realized that the girl had such a tempting mouth? She stretched up her lithe body to him, and he bent to her. He kissed her and she warmly returned the kiss, though not with an excess of fervour which he might have found alarming.

He had loved many women in his day, and it was true,

as Joan said, he thought exultantly, that he was not yet too
old for such delights. He chuckled when she told him so, finding her charmingly naïve and flattering, and was emboldened
to fondle her.

'You're wonderful,' he told her.

Joan was secretly amused, but she, too, was flattered. He
must have been well worth while twenty years ago, she
thought, and even now he wasn't too bad. He'd marry her
and make a lady of her, and it was true that he was still
handsome. She'd be Clare's equal and Geoffrey would have
to treat her as such, not that she'd be likely to see much
of them, but no doubt there'd be occasional meetings. It
did not occur to her that Noel would expect her to be faithful to him, that would be too much for sixty-odd to ask of
a girl in her twenties, but she'd be discreet as she always had
been, and would value her status as a married woman. In
promising to care for him, to cherish him, she was perfectly
sincere. It had been a pleasure for her to look after his clothes
and see him spruced up and looking distinguished; and this
would be intensified when he was her husband.

More than once the fleeting thought had struck Joan that
there were advantages in being an old man's darling, but
nevertheless she had not seriously thought of cozening a
proposal of marriage from Noel until this evening. For this
her chagrin at Geoffrey's dismissal was responsible. Her
overture had been an impulsive one, but she did not regret
it. Indeed, with every moment that passed, she became more
aware of the advantages of such a marriage. Presently she
was sitting in his lap, and her arms were round his neck.

'Never tell me again that you're too old,' she chided indul-
gently, and was not unprepared for his fatuous reply : 'You'll
make me young again, my pet.'

'You won't let me go away alone tomorrow, will you?' she
coaxed.

'But need you go now, dearest girl? Wait until Clare and
Geoff return, and then we'll tell them.'

'Oh no, no, though it's sweet to think you want to – but
it would be so awkward for them. They'd feel they had to
make objections. Come with me, and then we'll write to them

and tell them we're married. It could be in a few days' time, couldn't it?'

'I don't see why not. A special licence wouldn't be too much of an extravagance. But how could I leave so soon? All my belongings . . .'

'I'll pack for you tonight. I rang up for a car to take me to the station for the early train tomorrow morning, and we can go together. Nobody will know until we are well on the way to London. We can stay at a quiet hotel, just for a few days until we find rooms or a house, and then your furniture can be sent on to London.'

It wasn't a bad idea, Noel thought, and it would mean he need not see Angela again. He hadn't the least idea what she intended to do, but thought it unlikely that she would make trouble for him if he left 'Welcomes'. What she had said was inexplicable and mysterious, but she had given the impression of not being personally interested in the theft of his late wife's pearls.

'I should have to take some of my treasures with me,' he said, glancing towards the cabinet. 'They comprise part of our capital, you know.'

'Are those things worth a lot?'

'They are. I've picked up some good pieces, besides many which were left to me. Sold to the right people they should bring in a substantial amount.'

'I can pack some of them, the ones which you select,' said Joan. 'And there's your book – that'll make money too, won't it?'

'Probably. There's a market for such work, and Quentin's name is still remembered, but I'm a slow worker and it hasn't been easy to do research work here.'

'It'll be better in London, won't it? And I'll see you have a lovely, peaceful time. How proud I'd be, if I were the wife of a famous author.'

'Perhaps you will be, my dear,' and Noel smiled with self-satisfaction.

Joan slid off his knee and said practically, 'If we're to get away early, I'd better make a start on the packing. I can get your cases and trunks out of the box-room while everyone is downstairs and not thinking of us. I'm supposed to be having a rest, for Miss Redcliffe wanted me to take a hand at cards, and I said I was too tired – so she won't bother me again. What about you getting into bed, while I see about cooking you a bit of supper? And then you can go off to sleep and I'll be as quiet as I can, while I pack for you.'

'But my poor child, it will take you half the night,' Noel said with concern.

'As though I mind! I can do without much sleep for once, but I won't let you knock yourself up – not now especially, when you belong to me.'

She was beautiful, thought Noel. Excitement had kindled a glow in her eyes and a bright colour in her usually pale cheeks. Feeling masterful and triumphant, he drew her back to him for a further embrace, and said : 'You shan't regret this, Joan. Everything I have will be yours, and as I've told you – as you shrewdly guessed, I'm not as poor as I'm supposed to be. I'd a certain amount salted away even when my wife was alive. She was as mean as charity, but – well – she did occasionally shell out, though I didn't feel called upon to tell anyone here that I had more than the trust fund.'

Joan nodded understandingly. Of course there'd be pickings for any man who married a rich wife, and why not? Noel would have been a fool if he hadn't looked out for himself.

'It might even run to a sable wrap for you, if not a coat, later on,' Noel said fondly.

Joan regarded him thoughtfully for a minute, and then she said, 'I'm not marrying you for that – not really. If you hadn't a bean I wouldn't risk it; I wouldn't with any man, but you're the right sort, saving and sensible, and I like you, and I mean it when I say I shall be proud . . .'

The odd thing was that she was sincere, for she realized that, with her roving, desirous temperament, it was unlikely she could have made a successful marriage with a man of her own age, who would be jealously observant of her. But with Noel, her dual nature would find scope and satisfaction. She was a natural housewife, and would be proud of her home and of him; she would be thrifty and ambitious, and when she craved for excitement, well, that could be gratified easily enough, and without causing the poor old thing any distress, for she would see to it that he never suspected it.

7

In the train on their homeward way, with a first-class carriage to themselves, Clare sat close to Geoffrey, her hand in his.

'I wish we could have stayed away for a week or more, she said. 'It was such a short time to be free, by ourselves, able to forget them all.'

To which Geoffrey retorted, 'It was you who insisted on returning. I'd have skipped this wretched party. I could have written and made a plausible excuse.'

'Nichol would only have put it off. We should have had to face it sooner or later.'

'For the life of me I can't see why. We're not forced to dance to his tune. He's an agreeable chap, but we've only known him for a few weeks.'

'I have the feeling that we couldn't have evaded it,' Clare said. 'It's as though we have to go through with it.'

Geoffrey put his hand under her chin and turned her face to his. 'Relax,' he said. 'What's troubling you? I thought nothing had, for the last few days.'

She sighed nostalgically, and then smiled. 'No, we've been gloriously happy, happier than I thought anyone could be, but today . . . I've hated today. From the moment we left the hotel, I've dreaded coming home.'

'But why on earth? If anything disastrous had happened, somebody would have sent a telegram.'

'I suppose so.'

Geoffrey eyed her uneasily, for in this mood she was strange to him. Moreover he knew, or thought he knew that it would be a shock to find Joan had gone. It was as though she had some psychic prescience of this; but even so, Joan's presence or otherwise was not sufficient to account for her white face and heavy eyes.

'It's all right – nothing really,' Clare said with a slight shiver. 'I don't know why I'm feeling so – so peculiar. I've been fighting it all day, but I'm goosefleshy. A sort of a cold tingle all over.'

'Nerves,' Geoffrey decided. 'Say the word, and when we arrive, we'll go straight back again.'

'That wouldn't be a bit of good. I know I'm absurd. Don't take any notice of me . . . we've had such a lovely time. Why had it to come to an end?'

'It needn't. I've told you that. It *was* a second honeymoon, wasn't it?'

'Much, much better than our first. Geoff, I did love you so.'

'Why the past tense? You won't stop loving me, now that we're home again, I hope.'

'No . . . oh Geoff!'

He laughed, though with some exasperation. 'It's lucky it's nearly dark, and that we have the compartment to ourselves, for I know of only one way to deal with you,' he said, and pulled her into his arms.

Kisses which were more rough than tender evoked a satisfactory response, and he said, 'Still got the gooseflesh sensation?'

'It's not so bad now. We can face things together, can't we? But how I wish we were returning to an empty house. It's hateful of me, but the others spoil it to some extent, even Angela – though I'm fond of her.'

'Well, at least she is not a fixture, and if we were sufficiently resolute we could make other arrangements for the old people.'

'But we're not. We've talked that over often enough, and decided we can't turn them out.'

To Geoffrey's relief, her voice and appearance were more

normal, and she said, 'Of course we can't. I'm making a stupid fuss. It *is* our home after all, and I expect they'll be pleased to see us.'

Geoffrey looked at her doubtfully, and she knew he was dreading the moment when it would be broken to her that Joan had inexplicably departed. She wished she could reassure him, but it would be easier for them both if she acted surprised, and then later told him she was glad, and that she would enjoy managing on her own, and she was sure she would do well enough in time, if he would have patience with her.

But as it turned out there was no necessity to act astonishment.

'We've all had a terrible shock,' Becky said. 'It's useless to try to break it to you gently – such a thing can't be broken gently. Even I never suspected . . . it's Noel . . .'

'Noel and Joan,' chirped in Phillis.

Becky shrugged and said, 'You tell them, then.'

'They've eloped,' Phillis announced, astonished but pleased to be given this dramatic opportunity.

Becky willingly allowed her to be the narrator. For once she was not voluble. The shock had been great and her disapproval was unmitigated. Noel, she remarked, must be out of his mind, in his dotage, and should be certified.

'Oh Becky, say what you will, it *is* romantic,' Phillis said.

'Romantic! A man of Noel's years marrying a chit in her twenties – and a servant. To my mind it's disgusting.'

'Joan is old for her age,' Clare said, 'and she isn't just a little village girl in her first place. She's sufficiently intelligent to adapt herself to any environment.'

This was her first contribution to the conversation, and Becky attacked her sharply. 'You surely don't approve? Noel has made fools of us all. I twitted him with having a penchant for the girl, but I didn't seriously believe it. Now I suspect they've been having an affair for ages.'

'We've no right to think that,' Clare said and then asked: 'Did either of them leave a message?'

'Two letters – both from Noel,' Becky told her. 'One to me, and one to you. I dare say they're both much the same.

He wrote me tersely enough that he and Joan were leaving, and would be married by special licence. He hoped by the end of this week.'

'But Noel's so poor. How will they live?' Phillis wondered.

'There's his jade collection,' said Becky. 'He told everyone it wasn't of much value, and I believed him, knowing Isabel wouldn't have left it to him if it had been. But I suppose it might be worth a few hundred.'

'Much more than that,' Angela said.

At this, they one and all turned to look at her, and Becky said, 'How do you know?'

'He showed it to me yesterday. I'm not an expert about jade, but my ex-husband was, and I picked up knowledge from him. Some of Mr Moore's pieces were good, very good indeed.'

'Then Joan may not have done so badly for herself,' Phillis said. 'But, oh dear, she was really invaluable. What will you do without her, Clare?'

'I shall manage,' Clare replied. 'Things won't be run as smoothly for a little while, but I shall learn.'

Later, when they were able to escape to their own room, Geoffrey said, 'You took that very well, but until you get used to doing without her, it will be hard for you.'

'It'll be worse for you. Joan was not only our housekeeper, but your personal attendant. I shall do my best, but I haven't her natural talent for home-making and valeting.'

'You won't be required to valet me. I can look after myself – could have done all along, only she happened to be there. Still, it's an upset for you, and a shock . . .' and suddenly he chuckled. 'I've never before seen poor old Becky thoroughly scandalized.'

'It must have been Joan who thought of it,' mused Clare. 'I'm sure the idea of marriage would never have occurred to Uncle Noel. Can it possibly turn out well, do you think?'

Geoffrey shrugged. 'Your guess is as good as mine, but – poor old chap!'

'Joan's such a strange girl, but she does like looking after people, and she's a wonderful manager.'

'Yes – from that angle, marriage between such a girl and an elderly man is not unpromising,' Geoffrey admitted.

'Well, it's their own affair. The snob part of it – Joan being a different class seems unimportant to me, though it's what chiefly outrages Becky. You sometimes said Joan was a dark horse, but it appears as though Uncle Noel is a dark horse as well.'

'Come to think of it, we never really knew much about him,' Geoffrey said. 'We thought him a harmless dabbler, with his biography and his old-maidish fussiness, but there must be much more to him than that.'

'Becky,' said Clare, 'accused him of being an old Don Juan, but that seems so absurd and somehow horrid; though surely he can't be in love with Joan – I mean really in love.'

'Heaven help him if he is!'

Clare did not ask for an explanation; she did not need one, did not want Geoffrey to be more explicit. Although astounded and bewildered by this new event, she already sensed that, so far as they were concerned, the strange marriage might be no bad thing. Secretly they would both have worried over Joan and her subsequent fate, but now this was settled, and perhaps not unsatisfactorily.

Geoffrey, for his part, was remembering uncomfortably and vividly the scene with Joan, which might have brought disaster upon him. What on earth would poor old Noel make of such a tigress, unless their marriage was to be a platonic one? But realizing something of the old man's vanity, he doubted if he contemplated any such thing, and Joan was too clever to disillusion him. She'd play up to him.

For himself, he was immensely thankful that she was now miles away. It could well be months, years even, before they saw her again.

Clare said, 'Uncle Noel, in his letter, asks me to keep his things until he can give me an address where they can be sent. They plan to live in London. It's such a feeble, silly sort of letter, all about Joan's perfections, and how proud he will be to call her his wife.'

'One can but hope he'll continue to think so when the first raptures are over. I suppose we'd better write and wish them happiness.'

'How can we? We don't know the address. We must wait until we hear again.'

'Let's look on the bright side,' Geoffrey suggested. 'You're at least free of one of your dependants.'

'And of Joan as well,' Clare said incautiously.

There was a moment of silence, and then Geoffrey swung her round to face him. He said, 'Are you glad to be rid of her?'

'Yes – I . . . oh, I don't know. Let me go, Geoff. I haven't finished unpacking the cases.'

'They can wait. Tell the truth. You *are* glad.'

'Well, if you must know, I think she was getting too fond of you. It isn't important. I mean I'm sure it meant nothing to you.'

'Yes, you should be sure of that,' he said quietly.

'But I naturally wouldn't have wanted her around. Nor would you. I'd hate to think anyone else was trying to attract you. I dare say lots of women will, but not under my very nose.'

'I shouldn't notice it, not even if it were under *my* nose. Is this a sign of jealousy? If it is I welcome it. I could be madly jealous if you showed any signs of interest in another man.'

'There's nothing less likely,' she said. 'You are my whole world, though I doubt if you were until this week-end.'

'You loved me, didn't you?'

'Yes – but incompletely, for sex is important and a part of love, isn't it?'

'Yes,' Geoffrey said, watching her.

'It's as though I didn't realize it. At the start I was confused and nervous, and then it became a kind of duty, though meaningless to me. I yearned for you to be just an affectionate companion. There was nothing attractive to me in the act of love.'

'You're a primitive creature,' Geoffrey said. 'It wasn't only because I denied you conception, but because to play safe doesn't excite you. Even if you didn't want children, you'd find stimulation in the element of chance.'

'I dare say there's some truth in that,' Clare agreed.

But it wasn't all the truth, though she had no words to describe her satisfaction because surrender was now as much on his side as on hers. Under such conditions she had discovered new powers in herself; an unsuspected capacity for enjoyment and a generous desire to give. Rather diffidently she questioned him.

'Did I please you?'

'You did. Were you happy?'

'You know the answer to that. Oh Geoff, I always knew that any other woman would have found you a wonderful lover. It was partly my fault. I hated the compromise so much that I made myself not want you, but you wouldn't have compromised for ever, would you – not even for very much longer?'

'No,' Geoffrey answered, his surrender complete.

*

Nichol called at 'Welcomes' that evening, and found Angela and Phillis alone. Becky had gone early to bed, and Geoffrey and Clare were out, paying a call on a friend in the village, who was ill. Angela had agreed to keep Phillis company while they were away.

'Dear me, how nice to see you,' Phillis said, 'though I was just about to go to bed. We've had an exciting day – not altogether pleasurable, but still . . .'

'I heard about it,' Nichol said. 'That was why I called round. I was afraid you might want me to cancel my little party tomorrow.'

'Oh no, I'm sure none of us would want you to do that,' said Phillis emphatically. 'We're all looking forward to it, even though we shall be a man short. But that doesn't matter so much for a buffet party. When you say you've heard – does that mean the news is all round the village – already?'

'Not so far as I know. You, yourself, my dear lady, were responsible for the story reaching my ears. It seems you met my man this morning in the village, and told him what had happened.'

Somewhat abashed, Phillis owned that she had. 'I was really so agitated, so upset, especially as Geoffrey and Clare

were away, and we dreaded breaking the news to them, and
then I came face to face with your manservant, so superior
and really so sympathetic, and he recognized me – from years
ago, I mean, when I was on the stage and much younger.'

'Really? Was he a fan of yours?' Nichol asked.

'He says he was. It seems he was in a home or hospital
of some kind, poor fellow, and the company with which I was
playing gave a performance of a play there. I remember it
well. It was *Lord Grangefield's Wife,* and I was the wife.
Such a sweet part.'

'But do you remember giving this special performance?'

'No, I can't say I do – but then we often did that sort
of thing for charity. George Dennesley was the manager, and
he went in for good works, and so the company had to do
the same. But really, when I heard how much your man had
enjoyed my acting and how he had never forgotten me, I
did feel touched and pleased. It seems I gave him my auto-
graph, and he has always kept it.'

'I had no idea Links was such a sentimentalist,' Nichol
observed.

'An actress does appreciate that sort of thing,' Phillis
said. 'It's nice to know I've changed so little, and that he
recognized me. Though it was only about ten years ago,
nobody thought I looked too old for the part.'

'No doubt you could play it tomorrow with equal success,'
Nichol said charmingly. 'If you were really going off to
bed when I arrived, don't let me keep you up from your
rest.'

'I certainly did think I'd have a long night after such a
day. I do hope you don't think it was indiscreet of me to
tell your manservant what had happened. He realized that
I was nervous and even a bit tearful, and he asked me, well,
he persuaded me to allow him to take me into The Crown
Hotel for a glass of wine. I know it wasn't quite the thing,
but I certainly was in need of a pick-me-up.'

'I think it was rather sweet of Links,' Angela said. 'You
must have made a big impression on him.'

Phillis giggled happily. 'It does look like it, doesn't it?'

Another ten minutes passed before she got through the

motions of departure, but at last she fluttered away, and Nichol said: 'That's fortunate – fortunate, too, that the Deerings went out. It might have been a bit difficult to get you alone.'

'Difficult for *you*?'

He retorted impatiently, 'Do remember that it's necessary for me to act as a perfectly ordinary human being. Were others present, I could scarcely command you to take me to your room for a private conversation.'

'They'd certainly think there was something between us.'

'As there is.'

'But not that sort of something. Now I come to think of it – I wonder – have you ever, with any woman? Would you descend to being *that* human?'

'That's no concern of yours.'

'It isn't, but it's an intriguing speculation.'

'Stop fooling – and listen to me.'

'Oh, very well,' Angela agreed, 'but there was a certain amount of fooling when we first met, and in those days I liked you. I thought you an amusing rattle. What an idiot I was.'

'You're acting far more stupidly now. I'm forced to remind you that you can't afford to adopt such a tone. Things here have taken an unexpected turn. What's at the back of it all? Why did that old fool go off with the girl?'

Angela opened her eyes wide and said innocently, 'How should I know?'

'If you've bungled matters, you may be sorry for it. I had almost said you may live to be sorry for it, but that's problematical as you realize.'

'Be fair,' Angela said. 'You told me yourself that I was only required to do my best, and I have done my best. How on earth can you make me responsible for Noel Moore's elderly yearnings? I hadn't the slightest idea there was anything between him and the girl.'

'Then "the sight" has failed you of late.'

'It never worked that way; warning me in detail what people would do, or who they liked or disliked. It was always a chancy thing. But, by and large, I generally saw if anything beastly was going to happen to a person; that's why I got the name for being unlucky; a Jonah. I was in three touring companies which went broke on the road, and I was prepared for it. But as for Noel Moore, all I thought was that he was a fussy, tiresome old bore, and nobody was more surprised when I heard he'd done a bolt with Joan.'

'You've fallen down on every one of your assignments so far,' Nichol said.

'How have I? I've followed instructions. I found the secret drawer and the diary, though what it contained I haven't a notion—nothing radically harmful from the look of things. Poor old Phillis is too fond of the bottle, and I've dropped a few useful hints around, or they should have been useful, but Clare's dense, and I doubt if Geoffrey even listened. When he's not absorbed in her, he thinks of nothing but his music. I told Clare that I suspected he was having an affair with Joan, but far from causing a breach, it seems to have welded them together; and now the girl's gone and no longer a problem to either of them.'

'What about the pearls?' Nichol asked.

It was Angela's instinct to avoid his eyes, but this would almost certainly arouse suspicion, so she forced herself to glance up casually, as she said, 'That's a wash-out. Noel knows nothing about them.'

'Absurd! I was given definite information.'

'Your definite information was wrong, or I'm pretty sure it was. The poor fool hasn't anything but his miserable trust, and it beats me how he and Joan will manage on that. She'll go out to work, I suppose, and think it's worth while because a so-called gentleman has put a ring on her finger. I've combed his room when he was out, and looked through his cheque-book stubs and seen the miserable little sums he takes out of the bank from time to time; and I've got on his right side and he's shown me all his treasures. Those pearls could have been stolen by at least a dozen domestics who worked for his wife, which the family know : that's why they never actually accused Noel. Certainly he didn't get hold of them. I should know if he had—I could sense a thief or a murderer if I were within touch of one. Noel Moore's not a thief though, as Becky Redcliffe says, he may be an old Don Juan.'

Nichol was silent, but his gaze was fixed on her, and she felt shrinkingly that he was doing his best to read her mind and drag forth its smallest secret. Triumph, which she sedulously suppressed, flared within her as she realized that he was powerless to do so, for there was no mistaking his disappointment as he said, 'I should have thought myself it was an outside chance if I hadn't been given this information.'

'You can scare people into telling lies as easily as you can scare them into telling the truth,' said Angela.

She was silently wondering. Why didn't he realize that it shouldn't be necessary for him to rely on information? Why didn't he know that Noel had stolen the pearls and camouflaged certain of his jade specimens? He had known about the secret drawer in the desk, and possibly the contents of the diary. He had known that Joan would try to seduce Geoffrey, then why . . .?

'You can write Noel off,' she said confidently, 'and the girl also. They'll go to the devil in their own way.'

*

Angela only realized how much the interlude with Nichol had shaken her, after he had left her. She had won a trick, or so she believed, but she was not yet sufficiently sure to swing from fear to confidence.

It was fear which haunted her dreams that night; fear of Nichol's wrath if he discovered she was no longer his obedient discipline; and in the small hours of the morning, as she broke from a nightmare of horror, it was with a loud cry which rang piercingly through the house, and awoke both Geoffrey and Clare.

'It's Angela,' Clare cried, springing up in bed.

'What on earth's wrong?' Geoffrey, confused with sleep, was at the door, switching on the lights in the bedroom and the passage.

'She's had a nightmare or she's ill. Nobody has broken in. You needn't search for a weapon.'

This, in fact, was what Geoffrey was doing, for to him the

wild scream suggested a violent assault. But as Clare, pulling on her dressing-gown, ran along the passage, he, after a moment's hesitation, followed her. He stood in the doorway of their guest's room as Clare ran in, and heard sufficient to reassure him, before he returned to bed.

'I had the most dreadful dream,' Angela said, as Clare went to her. 'Did I make a noise and wake you? I'm so sorry.'

She was trembling violently, and although there were beads of sweat on her brow, she was very cold. Clare switched on the electric fire, chafed Angela's hands, gave her a drink of water, spoke to her soothingly. Although she had thought lately that she would be glad when Angela left, uncomfortably aware that there was something eerie about her, she was now thankful she had been within hearing. How awful if Angela had been by herself in a hotel, or even in a flat of her own, with nobody there who knew of all she had gone through. She had had frightening dreams for the first few nights after the shipwreck, but none of late, and the recurrence of such a dream and evidently a horrible one, was a matter for concern.

'I'm all right now,' Angela said. 'I do apologize . . . please, Clare, go back to bed. I'll keep the light on. I can't say I fancy the dark again.'

'It won't be long before it *is* light,' Clare comforted. 'But now I'll make some tea. No – really . . .' as Angela protested. 'I'd love some myself, and I'll take Geoff a cup.'

'Did I wake him as well? Oh dear!'

'That scream of yours would have wakened anyone sleeping in this part of the house, but fortunately they don't. Will you be all right while I go downstairs to put on the kettle, or shall I tell Geoff to come and sit with you?'

'Of course not – but leave the door open.'

By the time Clare returned with a tray, poured out a cup of tea and took it to Geoffrey, and then came back to Angela, she was looking much as usual.

'I suppose you dreamed of the shipwreck,' she said.

'That and other things. Poor Clare, I'm an uncomfortable guest, but I shan't be here much longer.'

'I'd far rather you stayed here until your nerves are stronger.'

'My dear, I may dream of horrors off and on for years. It's only to be expected, though I hope I shan't, if things turn out well – if I'm able to get away from here.'

This remark struck Clare as peculiar, and she sat down on the end of Angela's bed and said, watching her as she drank her steaming tea : 'What do you hope will turn out well – or fear will turn out badly? Why shouldn't you be "able" to get away?'

'If I told you, you wouldn't believe me, you *couldn't* believe me. It would make you feel uneasy, but you would dismiss it as fantastic and impossible.'

'I mightn't – or at least I might think as I *have* thought lately – that fantastic happenings aren't a bit impossible.'

'I would tell you a little, if I thought it would warn you. Perhaps I ought to try. But put into words, it'll sound stupid or melodramatic. If anything happens to me . . .'

'Nothing will happen to you. I'll see to that . . .'

Angela summoned up a weak laugh. 'You haven't the slightest idea what I mean, and yet, I do believe that if anyone could fight and win a battle with the powers of darkness, it would be you. If misfortune should happen to you, don't have anything to do with Nichol.'

'What *could* I have to do with him?'

'I don't know exactly, but he's attracted to you in the weirdest kind of way. I can't imagine him in love with anyone . . . but it's the attraction of opposites, and you do like him and find him fascinating.'

'Because he's unusual, but if you think . . .'

'Of course I know you're in love with Geoffrey, but he could have power over you.'

'Oh, nonsense, Angela. If he tried to impress me in any ridiculous way, well, it *would* be ridiculous, and I should laugh at him.'

'That mightn't be a bad thing. Laughter can be a weapon. Clare, he's an evil person.'

Her eyes were earnest and pleaded with Clare to believe her, and Clare gazed at her thoughtfully, and said, 'You've spoken like that before, or in something the same way. It seems absurd, for he appears to be charming, and harmless. But perhaps it's not absurd.'

'I swear to you it isn't. I don't know all there is to know about Nichol, not by any means, but I know enough to fear and hate him.'

'But he saved you, he brought you here; he talks as though he's your close friend, and you told me yourself how he helped you when you were having such a ghastly time with your husband.'

'He did, but as for friendship – I'd sooner be friendly with a boa-constrictor. Listen, Clare, he isn't a normal human being. He has strange – wickednesses; he has dabbled in all kinds of horrible cults, and he knows too much.'

'About you? About me?'

'I think he sees you as a traditional enemy, a natural giver of life and happiness. You represent fruitfulness, health, beauty, and wholesomeness. You have no place in the dark; his dark and mine. He'd be pleased to drag you down, to frighten you, to overawe you, make you plead with him or succumb. It would be a triumph if he could. Yet there's a tiny speck of his mind, which has a tormented love for you.'

'Angela!'

'It sounds sheerest nonsense, doesn't it?'

'I don't know – not exactly – but it's hateful.'

'Yes, it's hateful, but try to believe me. Don't be impressed by his good looks and his good manners and his interesting way of talking. You have protection in your own nature, which I never had; yet in the beginning, I too thought him charming and enjoyed his companionship. Now, I'm in his power, or he thinks I am, but in my mind there's the tiniest doubt, a glimmer of hope, and you can't imagine how wonderful that is.'

Against her will, Clare was impressed. She said helplessly, 'I don't know what to say – you frighten me – most of all when you suggest that something dreadful may happen to you.'

'But it may not. A week ago I was certain it would, but now

there's a hope.'

'Angela, you say Nichol is evil, and that he has done dreadful things. If that's true, are they the sort of things you could go to the police about?'

'Good heavens, no!' and Angela laughed wildly.

'Then I believe he's frightening you, and has made you believe all sorts of crazy things. I can imagine that he might, if you've quarrelled and he wants to pay you out.'

'He may have made me believe more than is true – oh God, I hope he has,' Angela's voice broke. 'But if he has, I shall know soon.'

Clare was worried. She said, 'I wish we needn't go to this party tomorrow night. Even if I felt quite comfortable about Nichol, I wouldn't want to. We've had too many upsets, and I'm not in the party mood.'

'We must go though,' Angela said. 'Then, perhaps, something will happen to end it all. I'm not sure – but I seem to see . . .'

Watching her, Clare saw her face sharpen, and in contrast to that sharpening, her eyes became huge and misty. She cried out in appeal: 'Don't, Angela – please don't! If you start to tell me what's going to happen in the future, I shall scream.'

Slowly, the look of unnatural perception faded from Angela's face, and she said, 'There's been enough screaming for one night. I'll tell you nothing more. Words are clumsy things, and events have a way of working themselves out. Go back to bed, Clare, I'm all right now, and I shan't dream again, even if I do fall asleep.'

'Very well, if you're sure you're not frightened any longer.'

'I'm quite sure. I'm sorry to have given you such a broken night, and thanks for the tea.'

*

Becky Redcliffe also had a restless night, but this was not due to a nightmare, but to the fact that her rheumatic pains were worse than usual. Marty, in her nearby room, heard Becky moaning and moving heavily, when she woke early in the morning, and she went to the old woman's room and said sympathetically, 'You look as though you've had little sleep. Why didn't you ring your bell, and I'd have made you a hot drink or given you some massage?'

'It wasn't more than I could put up with,' said Becky, 'and you do enough waiting on me in the daytime, without sacrificing your night's sleep.'

It was odd, as Marty often thought, that she should be considerate on this one point, when she was such a slave-driver in other ways. Marty could not remember that Becky had ever voluntarily awakened her at nights, though being a light sleeper, she had often wakened of her own accord.

'You shall have your breakfast early, and your massage early,' she said.

She dressed quickly, prepared the breakfast tray and brought it in, and then as Becky was lifting her tea-cup with both her crippled hands, they heard the postman's knock.

Hurrying out to him, Marty returned with three letters. Two for Becky and one for herself. Becky's were both illustrated catalogues from London shops and she was glancing through them when she became aware of Marty's utter stillness, and glanced up at her. 'What's the matter?' she asked.

Marty had not yet opened her letter and she was staring at the address on the envelope. She said in an odd voice, 'This has been sent from London, from our old address, your old address of three, or is it four years ago?'

'Nearer four. What is it? There's still the same head-porter and he'd readdress any letter which came to you or me.'

'I seem to recognize the writing,' Marty said in a choked voice. 'I'm not sure, but . . .'

'Well, don't stand there twisting and turning it about,' Becky said with asperity. 'If you open it, you'll soon find out who's written it.'

'Yes – that's true.'

'You've gone all colours. One might think you'd seen a ghost.'

'Perhaps I have.'

The words, 'Don't be a fool,' were on Becky's tongue, were

about to be spoken, and then she abruptly checked herself, and there was a touch of apprehension in her manner as she asked : 'It's got a foreign stamp on it, hasn't it?'

'American,' Marty said, and then turned upon Becky a look which, for her, was distracted. 'I'll read it in my room,' she said, and went off so blunderingly that she knocked against a small table, which tipped against a chair, and stayed in that position, for Marty did not set it upright again.

'Well, really!' Becky said, but there was more anxiety than annoyance in the exclamation.

Determinedly she drank her tea, spooned her cereal, munched the fingers of toast which Marty had cut and buttered; but they were tasteless to her.

It couldn't be that that creature had written after all these years. It was true he had gone to Canada, but there hadn't been a word from him since. She would have known if there had been, Marty would have told her. Even if he had, why should she worry? It was all past history, and everything settled for the best. It wasn't likely he'd mention what had happened, or mention her.

Nevertheless, as the minutes passed and Marty did not return, Becky's anxiety mounted, and at last she could bear it no longer. She stretched out her hand and rang the bell which was always within her reach. After a pause, Marty answered the summons.

'I've finished with the tray,' Becky said.

In silence Marty removed it, while Becky stole a side-glance at her. The silly creature certainly looked upset, her eyelids were reddened as though she had been crying. Becky wanted to ask questions, but found that she could not utter the words.

'Take your medicine,' Marty said, measuring it into a small glass.

To Becky, these words had an ominous significance, but she drank the dose, and watched Marty setting about the usual arrangements for her morning toilet.

The usual routine was carried out in complete silence, which was not usual. Becky ventured with a tart 'Have you lost your tongue?'

'I've things to think about. After I've given you your massage, I'll go out for a bit,' Marty said.

'It's a fine morning. You could wheel me along the cliffs.'

'It won't hurt you to stay in for once. Besides, I want to go down to the village.'

Marty spoke calmly but decisively and Becky took this almost meekly. 'Oh, very well, but while you are there you can change my library books, and for the lord's sake bring me something better than a sickly romance.'

'I'll try to find something exciting. Are you ready now for your massage?'

Becky inwardly shrank as Marty's plump, firm hands ministered to her, but they were as little hurtful as possible. When she was installed in the wheeled chair, Marty pushed it near to the window where she could look out in comfort, and said, 'I may not be back for an hour or more. Shall I ask Miss Gage to sit with you?'

'No thanks. I shall have more than enough of that burbling fool this evening.'

'Have it your own way,' Marty said stolidly, without expression.

The feeble tears of age, and not only of age but of fear and guilt, suffused Becky's eyes, as she heard Marty moving about in her room, and finally listened to her footsteps going along the passage to the side door, which closed behind her. Never had she more bitterly chafed against her helplessness. If she had had the full use of her limbs, she would have gone after Marty, or she would have stopped her. She would have taken her by the shoulders and shaken some sense into her. She would have made her tell her the contents of that letter. Though perhaps she would have told her had she been asked, only Becky hadn't been able to bring herself to ask.

What had that creature written to her? What *could* he have written? But she wasn't certain the letter from America was from him. It was Marty's odd manner which made her suspect it.

As he hadn't any idea of what had happened, there was nothing to fear, Becky told herself, and yet . . . oh well, better face it, there was that talk she had had with him, which had been designedly misleading. But she had acted in Marty's best interests. The man was a weakling, he would never have been good enough for her, and Marty knew it. She hadn't really cared for him, or if she had, she'd got over it.

A nice life he would have led her, even if he had done what fools would call the 'right thing'. Anyway, he hadn't wanted to; he'd been relieved beyond words to be let off, and Marty had soon realized that it was all for the best.

She — Becky — had been her benefactress; yes, from first to last, she had been that, as Marty had owned more than once. Of course Marty was grateful to her. Why not? Anyone would have been grateful. The thing was that, if she ever heard Becky had seen the creature, had talked to him, advised him, it might be hard to persuade her of her goodwill.

The minutes crept slowly away. An hour passed; more than an hour. Becky began to whimper. 'Oh God, send her back to me, don't let her leave me. What should I do without her now — after all these years?'

It was as much as she could do not to burst into loud sobs of relief when at last she heard the outer door open and knew that Marty had returned.

8

None of Nichol's invited guests had ever crossed the threshold of Walnut Tree Cottage, a fact which was responsible for as much excitement as the actual prospect of the party.

So many sinister rumours had been spread around that nobody knew what to expect; certainly not the light, pleasant and casually luxurious setting in which they presently found themselves.

Evidently Nichol had had the cottage redecorated, which was extraordinary as he had been in residence for only a matter of weeks; though perhaps the manservant was a handy person with a pot of white paint and a brush.

White paint there certainly was, in addition to expensive ultra-modern furniture which had not been there during the unhappy lifetime of the previous occupants. In the largest downstairs room, there were chairs upholstered in red leather, a thick white carpet, and coloured prints at once bizarre and banal hanging on the walls.

Clare was disappointed, for banality was the last thing she expected from Nichol. She glanced at Angela, who looked amused. Most of the others were pleasantly impressed. Drinks were many and varied, some unknown to the far from sophisticated residents of Beechslope.

Links, the manservant, middle-aged and thick-set, correctly attired in a dark uniform, circled amongst the guests with a loaded silver tray, and for each there was an individual small gift. These were not received with any particular pleasure by the recipients.

The general, unuttered opinion was that such largesse was unnecessary and slightly bad form, for none of them would feel in the least inclined, even could they afford it, to entertain Nichol in a lavish manner.

Moreover, there was something curiously cynical in these miniature gifts. For the Vicar, who was Low Church, and who openly avowed his dislike of Popish trappings, there was an onyx bird-bath which looked singularly like a receptacle for Holy Water, and upon which hieroglyphics in an unknown language were traced; unknown, that is to say, to the lay members of the party, for the inscription plainly disconcerted the Vicar when he glanced at it. His wife, who had the reputation for being 'near' received a gold charm for a bangle in the shape of a cheque-book, and the bank manager and his wife, who were said to be on bad terms, were given twin silver ashtrays upon the rims of which were perched two turtle doves. Dr Irris found himself the possessor of a scalpel-like paper-knife, made of ivory and edged with garnets which suspiciously resembled drops of blood; and to his pretty sharp-tongued wife there fell a small brooch in chrysoprase designed to represent an asp.

Angela, as she glanced from one stupefied face to another, listened to unconvincing words of thanks, could barely repress her mirth. Standing beside Clare, she murmured in a low voice, 'Not exactly a pleasant party, for all its window dressing.'

'No.'

Clare's agreement was troubled as she glanced across at Nichol, who at the moment was dividing his attention between Becky and Phillis.

'These people won't stay long. He doesn't want them to,' Angela said. 'You'll see – they'll make a general exit as soon as they can. What sweet favour fell to your share? This was mine.'

She opened her hand and showed Clare the small object which lay in her open palm; a tiny pendant in the shape of an ebony heart. 'That's his estimate of me.'

'Give it back to him. Refuse to take it. It's horrid,' Clare said.

'It doesn't worry me,' Angela said lightly. 'In fact, Nichol's method of trying to affront or frighten us strikes me as crude and vulgar and rather stupid, but it's very pleasant to be able to think of him in such terms. Do show me what you were given.'

'It's quite harmless, but far too expensive,' Clare said. 'I think I shall get Geoff to return it – and his own favour, whatever it is.'

'Quite harmless too,' Angela said. 'A pinchbeck cigarette-holder in the shape of a conductor's baton. Of course the pinchbeck is designed to stab, but it's not likely Geoffrey will care.'

Clare showed her a pair of gold ear-rings simulating twin sheaves of wheat, and Angela said, smiling: 'Very appropriate for Demeter.'

'I never wear ear-rings, and Geoff never uses a holder. What did Cousin Becky get? Nothing to upset her, I hope. She's been looking off-colour all day.'

'A gold seal and the engraving is a whip – the obvious slave-driver symbol, and Miss Gage got a rather horrid little comfit box in malachite, the lid shaped as a skull – death and decay.'

'He *is* hateful,' Clare said, shocked.

'I'm glad you're convinced of that – at last. But, to me, as I've said, it all seems stupid, though I've a strong idea that this party is intended to be a show-down or a climax of some kind.'

'I wish we could leave at once – all of us,' Clare said indignantly, and tried to catch Geoffrey's eye from across the room, but he was deep in conversation with Mrs Irris.

'I don't think Nichol intends us to leave when the others do,' Angela said with a shrug.

*

'A queer party, this, and there's certainly what can be described as an atmosphere,' Dr Irris observed to Geoffrey. 'The kind which, as people say, can be cut with a knife.' And then he added with a grin : 'Though that's a phrase of which I should be wary, as I'm a medico, and a blood-thirsty one if the gifts we have received tonight are intended to be signs and portents.'

'The whole thing is in vile taste,' Geoffrey said, 'but it's too absurd to give real offence, and why should the chap *want* to give offence? Why get people here who are friendly to him, in order to insult them expensively?'

'The Lord only knows, but he strikes me as a queer one. He's a foreigner of sorts, so I understand.'

'A mixture of several races, according to himself.'

'That accounts for it,' said Dr Irris in all seriousness. 'It wouldn't surprise me to find there was some kind of Socialist devilry at the bottom of this.'

'To do Nichol justice, I've never heard him touch on politics.'

'Too cunning, my dear fellow – they all are. He wouldn't open out here, because we're unpromising material. Beech-slope is a Conservative stronghold, as he's no doubt discovered. A Socialist candidate invariably loses his deposit.'

Geoffrey had the impulse to laugh. He found Nichol no more than ridiculous; but then so was Dr Irris. He was a short, plump man with small hands and feet of which he was patently vain. The hands were always white and mani-cured, the feet meticulously shod. His plump face normally bore some resemblance to a scone, thinly embedded with currants which had formed themselves into the pattern of eyes, nostrils and lips, but now that bleached countenance was a fiery red.

'He certainly doesn't rate us highly.' Geoffrey examined his pinchbeck baton with amusement. 'If he'd presented me with this a few weeks ago, I should have agreed with his estimate of me, but now I'm not so sure. I think I've done better work lately.'

'I shall throw this damned knife into the sea, on the homeward way,' Dr Irris said angrily, and Geoffrey realized that he had some cause for ire, since he had the reputation of consistently recommending surgical treatment even for minor and unimportant complaints. He continued to berate Nichol in an angry undertone. 'As for Miss Gage, to present her with that unpleasant-looking box is cruelty. Her heart is none too sound, and the shock of unwrapping the thing and seeing it, was enough to give her a dangerous attack.'

'Yes . . . poor Phillis,' Geoffrey agreed, sobered, 'but it didn't seem to upset her particularly. Nichol's manservant shared her indignation though, and took the thing away from her.'

'Well, that's very odd too,' Dr Irris said. 'Miss Gage was prattling about him being a fan of hers, which attracted my attention to the man, and I was immediately sure his face was familiar to me; but it's only a few minutes ago that I placed him. Believe it or not, that fellow has had a long sojourn in Broadmoor. Some years ago, I visited a medical colleague of mine who was attached to the place, and this fellow, Links, was one of the inmates. He'd been convicted of murder, but was found insane, and so escaped the death penalty, and my colleague aroused my interest by his opinion that his insanity was of a temporary nature, and that he would recover. It seems he was right.'

'Are you sure?' Geoffrey asked, startled, glancing at the man, who was hovering solicitously behind Phillis's chair.

'Positive. The Broadmoor fellow had a V-shaped scar on

his left cheek, and so has this chap.'

'He seems mild enough now, then, and certainly has protective instincts so far as Phillis is concerned.'

'It's fortunate for her, poor lady, that she's forgotten where that entertainment was given, which he reminded her about. It was Broadmoor. She'd have been very upset, if she had remembered.'

Geoffrey agreed, and the doctor said impatiently, with a glance at his watch: 'The sooner this so-called party comes to an end, the better. I've had enough, and fortunately, being a doctor, I can make a plausible excuse to leave early—a patient and a late call. I see that the Vicar has much the same idea, and I imagine his excuse will be a sick call. Break it up as soon as you can, Deering, that's my advice to you.'

He strutted across the room to collect his wife. Not a bad idea if he did the same by Clare, Geoffrey thought, but realized that it might be difficult to dislodge the two elderly women, who were apparently undisturbed by any sinister undercurrent. Becky was now talking animatedly to Nichol, and Phillis was queening it, enthroned in a high-backed chair, with Links in devoted attendance.

*

'Well, my lad,' said Becky, in high good humour, 'you've certainly given our friends and neighbours something to think about. A humourless lot they are. Now me, I've no objection to an expensive trifle emphasizing the fact that I know how to crack the whip, and as for Phillis—well, we all know what will be our ultimate end, so why should it upset her to see the reminder of it?'

'But to some,' Nichol said, 'the event will come sooner than to others, therefore it would perhaps have been tactful had that bibelot been bestowed on one of the younger members of the party. Angela, for instance, who this evening is so full of life and youth and high spirits.'

'Angela's black heart is sinister enough in all conscience,' Becky said with a cackle of laughter. 'Can it be that you have found her dark and treacherous in her dealings with you?'

'She can answer that,' Nichol said, 'but I regret you all

read such a personal meaning into my small gifts, which were intended to add a fillip to an occasion which might otherwise have bored.'

'Nobody has been bored, whatever else they may have been. Clare is the only one who has had a conventionally pretty present, and even hers – wheat, which could be symbolic of fruitfulness, and the poor child has been married unfruitfully for years.'

'Links has appropriated the little green skull,' Phillis said with a giggle. 'He actually asked me if I would allow him to buy me something else in place of it, as a souvenir of his admiration for a great actress. What do you think of that, Becky?'

'What I have always thought, my dear, that your acting talent, such as it was, was the type to commend itself to simple and uneducated members of the public.'

There followed the mutual glares, to which Geoffrey and Clare were well accustomed, and Nichol said, 'Links is brewing a brand of punch from a recipe which some time ago fell into my possession. It is said to have been a favourite posset with the ancient Romans. But the concoction takes a little time to prepare, and for the best effect the last ingredient must be added immediately before drinking.'

Geoffrey said, seizing the opportunity, 'A posset can be another word for stirrup-cup. It's time we were all making a move. Phillis, you, for one, are looking very tired.'

As a fact Phillis was sleepy. Her head was nodding, but every now and again she roused herself with a jerk. She had had several drinks, but although it was true, as Becky said, that spirits generally over-excited her, they had had little effect on her that evening. She did not guess that Links had mixed her drinks himself, and that they were innocuous ones.

Clare seconded Geoffrey, remarking that it was already past ten o'clock. Angela said nothing. She realized that it might not be easy for any of them to leave, simply because they now wanted to leave. Nichol's party had followed a devised plan, though she had no clear idea what it was.

'Let us all go into the other sitting-room, the one I use

135

when I am alone,' Nichol suggested. 'This room is so impersonal.'

Reluctantly, except for Becky, who was alight with curiosity, they followed his lead.

Phillis twittered, 'One might think you had bought all this lovely furniture just for this one occasion.'

'Perhaps I did,' Nichol said equably. 'I wanted it to be a success.'

'My dear boy, if you did, that was a plutocratic whim,' Becky said, 'though rumour has it that you *are* a plutocrat.' She cocked her head in a listening attitude. 'Dear me, is a storm getting up? The wind is whistling round the cottage, though I didn't hear it when we were in the other room.'

'But in this room it seems quite appropriate to hear the wind sighing,' Phillis said. 'What a complete contrast. Have you changed it much since you took possession?'

Nichol replied, 'Not very much, though I replaced curtains and carpets.'

These curtains and carpets were of a deep wine red, otherwise the room was barrenly furnished. There were ancient oak chairs and a settle; an inglenook fireplace; a beamed ceiling. A large fire was blazing, though this was insufficient to account for the stifling heat. The wind was now moaning eerily. The shuttered windows rattled, and the heavy curtain which covered the door was rippled as though by a strong draught.

'I don't think I like it,' said Phillis, in a voice which was suddenly shrill. 'Clare, can't we all go home?'

With relief, Clare replied, 'Yes, I think we should. As a storm has started, and we have to drive along the cliff, we shall be wise to go before it gets any worse, especially as Cousin Becky has to be carried to the carriage.'

'Clare, you're a spoil-sport,' Becky cried impatiently. 'I've left Marty with a face as long as a fiddle, though heaven only knows why, and I'm in no hurry to return to her.'

Nichol's glance flickered from one to the other. He said, 'When you have sampled what Geoffrey calls my stirrup-cup, I will speed you on your way. Here is Links now, and all that remains is for me to add the final soupçon to what is a rare brew.'

He went to a hanging cupboard, took a bronze flask from it, unscrewed the top and poured a few drops of liquid into the large, gilded punch-bowl, which Links put down on a table before him. Immediately the contents started to froth, and rose in a wave which threatened to curl over the edge of the bowl, while a blue haze filled the room.

At the general exclamation, Nichol said, 'Quite a dramatic effect, isn't it? But it's actually little more significant than the flicker of brandy flames around a Christmas pudding.'

He ladled the golden liquid, which appeared to be still smoking, into small bronze cups, and Links carried these round on a tray.

Nichol fixed his eyes on Angela, and as though compelled, she raised her cup to her lips. The others followed her example, with the exception of Clare, to whom at the moment nobody was paying attention. Her cup was set down untasted.

The effect of the drink was immediate, but varied. Becky sipped and sipped again with appreciation, then cackled with laughter as Geoffrey was seized by a fit of coughing. Angela, with a gasp, collapsed into the nearest chair, and Phillis said wonderingly, 'How dark it is! Why is it so dark? The room is full of shadows.'

'What on earth *is* this particular poison?' Geoffrey demanded, still coughing. 'It might be liquid fire.'

'Perhaps it is,' Nichol said quietly.

'I can't move,' Angela uttered the words in a choked and terrified voice.

'Really?' Nichol observed her with genial interest. 'But don't let that distress you. I shall be only too delighted for you to stay here – indefinitely. The rest of you can now return home.'

Phillis, with her bronze cup still in her hand, moved close to him. She said, 'There's a woman standing behind you; a strange woman. She came out of the shadows. What does she want?'

Her old, foolish, still pretty face bent to Nichol's face, and with a swift movement, he raised his hand and struck her across the cheek. 'Deering, take this maudlin creature home,' he commanded.

Phillis seemed to be unaware of the blow. She said earnestly, 'The woman thinks you killed her, or made somebody else kill her. She says she was thrown down the stairs. But you wouldn't do that – would you?'

Clare, clear-headed but terrified, wanted to scream. What had happened to them all? It was as though they had gone worlds away from her. They were demented, possessed, and she alone was sane.

Becky's exhilaration had vanished. She was murmuring one word, one name, repeatedly, 'Marty – Marty,' and then, 'Marty, don't leave me.'

Oh, if only Marty *were* here, thought Clare distractedly. Her robust common sense would have been welcome.

Phillis was smiling and bowing to the air, talking animatedly to a shadow whom nobody else could see. Geoffrey had torn off his collar. Angela sat paralysed.

'Go, the lot of you! Be off! I've done with you,' Nichol said imperiously.

Suddenly, inexplicably, Clare was no longer frightened and she laughed. 'It might be a scene from *Alice*,' she cried, 'but we're not a pack of cards, we're real people, and when we go, Angela goes with us, for it's us she belongs to, not to you.'

'So!' Nichol said – a long-drawn-out sound, soft but curiously satisfied. 'I might have known, Demeter, that before the end you and I would cross swords.'

Clare's gaze was deliberate as it rested on him. It was also scornful. He was nothing much, that gaze said; a fair, slight man, with bright, dark, pebble eyes. She, usually so kind and gentle, greatly desired to make rude, uninhibited remarks about those unpleasant eyes. As a child she had been embarrassingly outspoken, and it was as though she had forgotten the years between.

'A posing fool, aren't you?' she said. 'Acting as though you're a god, when all you did was to tip a drug into that bowl. But I didn't drink it, and the others will recover when they're in the open air.'

138

'Then get them out into the fresh air,' Nichol retorted. 'They've served my purpose. Angela now knows that I am not to be defied; that a contract must be honoured.'

'Oh Clare, don't argue with him,' Angela cried in anguish. 'Go, while you can, while you are all safe. I did make a bargain with him. I sold myself to him.'

'Sold yourself! He's not your lover, is he?'

'No. Not my lover, nor any woman's . . . but I did sell myself. I should have drowned, but he offered me my life in return for my services, and my soul.'

Clare stared incredulously. She said, 'Don't tell me you believe such rubbish. As though you *could* sell your soul, even if you were willing. For one thing it's not yours to sell, and for another, God wouldn't allow the devil himself to take advantage of a drowning girl's terrror.'

'He *is* the devil,' Angela whispered.

'That creature! That mountebank with his drugs and his conjuring tricks, and his petty spite!'

'Be careful,' Nichol warned.

Clare put her hands on her hips, threw back her head and laughed; rich, hearty, warm laughter, which splintered through the haze of that suffocating room.

'I suppose you call yourself Nichol because the devil is called Old Nick, but I doubt that if you ever come face to face with Lucifer, Son of the Morning, he will be bothered with you. Angela, get up at once, and come home with us.'

'Don't touch her!' Nichol rapped out.

'Oh, nonsense!' Clare stooped and made an attempt to pull Angela from her chair.

Nichol took a step towards her, and suddenly found Phillis clinging round his neck. 'I'm frightened of that woman,' she wailed. 'She says I'm not to let you go, that you belong to her.'

With a violent exclamation, Nichol pushed her aside, and Phillis screamed, whereupon Links, who had been standing in the background, threw down his empty tray and plunged forward.

'Leave her alone, you!' he growled. 'She's the pick of the

bunch, she is. Pretty as a picture she was years ago, when she and the others come down and acted for us; lifted all of us poor wretches out of the hell in which we were stewing.'

Phillis fell on her side as Links gripped Nichol by the throat. He shook him savagely, strangling the cry which the other uttered, but Becky, heaving herself to her feet, stood tottering, and her voice rang out with all the authority of one who was playing a leading part: 'You villain! Let him go!'

Phillis raised herself on her elbow and staggered up. 'That woman doesn't want him to go. She says the cottage is hers, and he's to stay here with her husband,' she cried. And then more plaintively: 'I wish you'd speak up. I'm not deaf, but you mutter so. What is it you want me to do? Oh, I see . . . well, yes, I suppose I can, if that's what you think advisable.'

Clare shivered, for this was frightening and horrible, if Nichol was not. She shrank, as the old woman brushed past her, and now in need of help she turned to Geoffrey. 'Can't you do something?' she entreated.

It was as though her appeal roused Geoffrey from a deep sleep. He rose, put his arm round her, and said as he stifled a yawn: 'My dear, it's time to be getting home. The party is over.'

Bewildered afresh, Clare gazed into his undisturbed eyes, which saw nothing of the scene around them. For him, the struggling, panting men, Becky enacting some long forgotten stage-part, Angela, sitting paralysed, and Phillis in converse with a phantom, did not exist.

'Wake up, oh please wake up,' Clare cried.

Geoffrey smiled. 'Surely it's not as bad as that . . . I wasn't actually asleep, dull party though it is.'

Clare turned from him in despair to watch Phillis, who, avoiding the two wrestling men, had glided across the room to clasp her arms around the gilt punch-bowl, still half-filled with the drugged liquor.

'Darker and darker,' Phillis complained, 'and she says there must be light.'

140

In her thin arms, she raised the bowl on high, and with a shrill cry of triumph, flung its contents into the glowing fire.

On the instant, the room was ablaze, and Clare as she screamed, heard Nichol also scream; a piercing cry of agony and horror, as with Links's hands still on his throat, he lurched backwards into a flaming cauldron.

*

There was rain, there was a cold, bitter wind, there was soft turf. Clare knew she was lying on the grass verge of the cliff, and she was holding Angela in her arms.

They were clasped close, and they were alone, but not for long. Geoffrey was speaking to her. There were other voices also, many voices. Clare heard Becky say imperiously: 'Give me your arm, my good man, and then I can get to the carriage. Once I am settled there, I beg you to attend to my poor friend, Miss Gage, who is in far worse case than I.'

Clare, though aware that Geoffrey was bending over her, was unwilling to open her eyes. A bright light was piercing her closed lids, and she knew that it was the light from the burning cottage.

'How did we get out of that awful place?' she asked. 'Did you carry us out?'

'I must have done.' Geoffrey seemed puzzled. 'I know I went back for Becky and Phillis and found them half-stifled in the hall.'

'Is Angela alive?'

'Darling, of course she is. You're holding her.'

'Yes—but I wasn't sure. Is she burnt?'

'Not a mark on her. She's sleeping peacefully, as you were for a few minutes. Clare, open your eyes and look at me.'

'Not to see the cottage burning. Please, Geoff . . . is the carriage near? Carry Angela, and I'll walk with my eyes closed. I can hold on to you.'

Geoffrey did not argue with her. He raised Angela in his arms, and Clare clutched his coat. The carriage was only a few yards away, and two fishermen from the village were lowering Phillis into it. Becky was already installed, calm and sitting upright.

'A most extraordinary experience,' Becky said. 'Alarming, though I've never felt less alarmed. They won't be able to save the cottage.'

Geoffrey glanced back at the flames leaping towards the sky. The fire brigade and hoses were turned upon the small building. A shout went up as the roof collapsed. Phillis was weeping softly, and Angela was still unconscious.

'Those two men. Could nothing be done?' Becky asked.

'They were blazing like torches,' Geoffrey answered curtly.

Becky groaned with exasperation. 'I wish I could remember what really happened. I seemed to be on the stage – my early days – in a small, stifling theatre . . . and a bad play, as I remember it. A melodrama.'

'They're all together now,' Phillis said between her sobs. 'It's what that woman wanted . . . to have them with her. She was murdered, of course, but she does seem to have had a nasty, revengeful nature . . . I mean when you're dead surely you should forgive your enemies, and after all what had Nichol done to her – or poor Links?'

'Oh, grant me patience,' Becky besought. 'She's out of her mind. There was no other woman there, Phillis, nobody but Clare and Angela.'

'Of course she was there. She told me to light up the scene and throw the stuff that was in the punch-bowl on the fire.'

'You might have killed us all,' Becky fumed.

'She saved us,' Clare said, 'or at the very least she saved Angela. Oh, I wish she would wake up. She couldn't move – she was paralysed.'

'Nonsense, nonsense,' Becky said. 'A young girl such as Angela wouldn't be likely to have a stroke. She fainted with fright, and small wonder. But, oh dear me, the tragedy of it . . . and only a few weeks after all those deaths in the storm. In a way poor Nichol brought it on himself, for goodness knows what was in that exceedingly odd punch he brewed. Everything was quite calm and pleasant until then, but after that . . . well, the stuff certainly went to my head, and as for Phillis, it sent her into a delirium.'

'I shall never drink anything stronger than water now –

never again, I swear it,' Phillis said.

'Let's hope you mean it,' Becky retorted tartly, 'for you've been a thorough disgrace for the last few years . . . all that cheap port too, nasty stuff! No wonder you could never hold down a job for any length of time.'

'It was my weakness, my dreadful weakness,' Phillis moaned. 'But I'm cured. I know I'm cured.'

'Well, if you are, that will be some good gained through this evening's tragedy.'

'That poor man. He gave his life for mine.'

'Well, yes, so he did,' Becky admitted, struck. 'He certainly saw something in you. Very odd.'

'He was a hero,' Phillis wept.

Clare stretched out her arm and put her hand on Phillis's knee. 'He was, Cousin Phillis,' she said gently. 'He's dead, but I'm sure he doesn't regret that he protected you – and all of us. He probably had a dreadful life, and isn't sorry it's over, and you were his ideal. If I were you, I wouldn't ever want to forget that.'

Geoffrey, who was driving, turned the horses into the open gates of 'Welcomes' and as he did so, Angela stirred, murmured something, and opened her eyes.

'Can you move? Do you think you can walk?' Clare said anxiously.

Angela looked at her wonderingly. 'Why not?' she asked.

When the horses pulled up and Geoffrey opened the carriage door, Angela rose, and disregarding Clare's outstretched hand, stepped lightly upon the pathway.

9

The burning of Willow Tree Cottage, the death of the men who had lived there, was a sensation which was never to be forgotten at Beechslope, and because there were rumours that before the catastrophe there had been odd doings at the cottage, the tragedy became one which with the passing of the years was embellished beyond recognition.

Evidence extracted at the inquest was obscure. Only Geoffrey, Angela and Clare were called as witnesses. The two old ladies were, according to medical reports, suffering from shock, and were not fit to attend. All Geoffrey could say, and in this he was supported by the two girls, was that Nichol had insisted on everyone tasting a special home-brewed punch, and that this concoction had had the effect of stupefying them all.

Geoffrey could remember nothing of what happened between drinking the punch and dragging the women from the burning house.

Angela described how she had been seized with some nervous paralysis, and Clare, who had not touched the drink and was therefore clear-headed, told the coroner that she had been terrified by the effect of the strange drink on her husband and her relatives, and especially upon Angela. She thought that Links, the manservant, was also upset, but about this she was confused; she only knew there had been a fight between the two men, that the bowl of punch had been upset, and that that was the start of the fire.

She was asked only a very few questions. The coroner, referring briefly to the ill-repute attached to the cottage, recommended the public to discount this as having any bearing upon the tragedy. He spoke of the tenant as a wealthy man who had travelled extensively, and remarked that the unknown liquor he had pressed upon his guests was indirectly responsible for later events. The jury brought in a verdict of accidental death, and the unrecognizable remains of the two men were buried in one grave.

The funeral attracted a crowd of sightseers, many living miles away, who afterwards repaired to the scene of the tragedy to view the spot where four violent deaths had now taken place.

But there was little to see, for the cottage was gutted, and only a pile of bricks and rubble and the blackened remnants of a garden remained.

144

Later, the wildest stories were to grow up around the place. Tales told by travellers, driving by at night, who reported that a fire was raging on the cliff, and from time to time it was said that cries and curses were heard by those walking on the sands beneath, and that figures were seen amongst the undergrowth, which soon grew unchecked.

Clare never voluntarily passed that way. 'Welcomes', fortunately, was nearly two miles distant, but even that was too near for her.

The house had lost its charm for her, and as she remarked to Geoffrey, there were disadvantages if one had a young family in living in a house on a cliff. Active boys and girls would be for ever scrambling up and down the steep pathways, hunting for seagulls' eggs in inaccessible spots, running risks.

'Sell the place, of course, if your heart is set on it,' Geoffrey said, 'though when you speak of our growing family, you are looking years ahead. It will take some time to produce your boys and girls, and an even longer time before they are beyond the toddling age.' And then he added with a smile: 'I know you hope you have already started a baby, and wouldn't be daunted if you were told that you could expect twins or triplets.'

'It would be wonderful,' said Clare, but scarcely expected his satisfactory words as he drew her to him.

'Yes, it would. I've come round to your way of thinking that the denial of life is a crime. We were both too near death, or worse, that evening. I felt it, though I can remember so little of what happened.'

'But I've told you what happened,' Clare said. 'Nichol got us there chiefly to demonstrate to Angela that we were all in his power, and she more than any of us.'

'In common with Becky, I can only say I wish I could remember what happened. I certainly failed to protect you.'

'But it wasn't your fault, and you saved us all in the end.'

'If only I hadn't touched that cursed stuff. For a moment it was agony; my throat burning and my head singing, and then, I suppose, I lost consciousness.'

'It was a dangerous drug,' said Clare. 'Becky went back

145

years in her history, to when she was first on the stage, and Phillis fancied she saw the ghost of the woman who was killed at the cottage. While as for Angela, she couldn't have been really paralysed, though she thinks she was. She is sure she was only freed after Nichol died.'

'Does she honestly believe he had supernatural powers?'

'Oh yes, but being herself an eerie sort of person, it's easy for her to believe that.'

'You're sceptical, aren't you?'

'I don't really know. It was all very queer, and I do feel that the less we think of it, the better. Our chief worry is with Becky and Phillis, who are both pretty low, and there's Angela, too – though she is full of life and hope, and will be leaving for London next week. I've become very fond of her. I hope the rest of her life will be peaceful and happy.'

'She's had a fright,' Geoffrey said, 'which probably won't do her any harm, for she got herself mixed up with some odd people, if Nichol is a sample.'

Clare made an evasive answer. There were certain aspects concerning Angela which she would never be able to discuss with Geoffrey, for they would only evoke his blank incredulity, though it might have been different had he been conscious during that short time when she, unaffected by the drug, had faced Nichol and had defied him.

Now her chief desire was to forget that nightmare, and she would, when Angela had left; when Becky and Phillis ceased to talk of it.

*

When Becky was brought home suffering from shock, Marty had cared for her, but with nothing of her old, spontaneous affection.

Between Becky and Marty there was a sense of strain and injury which neither made any effort to dispel.

Phillis claimed a certain amount of her time, and to her Marty felt much more sympathetic than to her autocratic employer, for Phillis insisted that she would never again touch a drop of liquor, and Marty, who was a lifelong abstainer, applauded her decision. She had nothing but pity for poor Phillis when she gave her the key of a locked cupboard

146

in her room, and Marty, on opening it, found that it was filled with empty bottles of the cheap wine which Becky had more than once scathingly referred to as 'her tipple'.

'The money I've wasted on the stuff, and now I know it was poison, absolute poison,' Phillis moaned to Marty and Angela. 'It made me deceitful and horrid, pretending as I did that I scarcely touched wine or spirits, while all the time I would be longing to get away by myself, longing to lock myself in and drink and drink. It was a craving, an irresistible craving, but now it's been scared out of me for ever. It's true, as Becky said, that I drank even while I was on tour, and of course it spoiled my work, and meant that I couldn't get the character parts in which I could still be good. But oh, my dears, it's a frightening thing to be growing old and to feel that one is lonely and unwanted.'

'You can't feel that way now,' Angela said, 'not when you remember how you saved my life.'

'But I can't remember much about that, and it doesn't seem to me that I did so much. It was poor Links who really destroyed that monster, and where he is now I tremble to think, though I am sure Links, in protecting me, redeemed himself.'

'I'm sure of it too,' Angela said, when she repeated this conversation to Clare. 'Whatever you may believe, I'm convinced that, but for Phillis and Links, I shouldn't be here today.'

'I sometimes think it would be helpful if we could get it all sorted out in our minds, but how can we?' Clare mused. 'Sometimes you seem to believe he actually was – if not Satan, a satanic being – but then again there are times when you jeer at him as a charlatan.'

'He was a mixture of both,' Angela said. 'But I know far too much which can't be explained. He was there on the ship that night, just as it was about to sink. Suddenly he was with me, and other people, who were drowned afterwards, also saw him and were tempted by him. He offered them all the chance of life if they would forfeit their hope of happiness in another world, but – people are wonderful, much more wonderful than one imagines. Nobody but myself accepted. They didn't want life on his terms, but I did.' And then as Clare was silent, she said with a sigh : 'But I know you don't believe me.'

'I do. At least I believe you think that was what happened. But it was no more than an awful dream, for how could he have been there on that sinking ship?'

'I don't know – but he was. He reminded me of it, afterwards. How I had accepted his terms, and was bound to him for ever.'

'He hypnotized you into believing you remembered. He was unscrupulous and wicked, and it pleased him to have you in his power. I don't deny he was – different – from other people, but he was human, just as you and I are human. He died, didn't he?'

'Yes, he died, and by the right death – by burning. You know it was always said that a witch could only be destroyed by fire, and the same thing must apply to a demon. It's all over. I'm not haunted by him. He's gone, and can never harm anyone again.'

'He couldn't have been destroyed, if he hadn't been an ordinary being,' Clare argued, 'but I never doubted that he was. To me there was something childish and ridiculous about him.'

'You made that plain enough when you stood up to him. How I admired you, and how frightened I was for you.'

'I was far more frightened for Phillis. She really *was* uncanny and horrible. He was no more than evil. And I admit he knew more about hypnotism than is generally known at present. It just happened that I was lucky enough not to touch that drugged liquor.'

'It was more than hypnotism,' Angela insisted. 'I know that, because I can sometimes see a little way into the future, and I realize he could see further. He told me about the secret drawer in the desk, and about the book which would be found there. He told me – certain things about Noel – about you all; even that Marty would have a letter which would cause some breach with Becky, and there *is* a breach between them; that's been obvious to us all.'

'I hope they'll come to an understanding,' Clare worried.

'I can't think what Becky would do without her.'

'They'll work it out, I dare say,' Angela said absently. 'You'd feel more at ease if you could convince me Nichol was a being straight from hell. I wonder why. It doesn't really matter now.'

'Probably because I hate you to think I was duped and deluded; a kind of conceit, for I'm a sane enough person as a rule.'

'Of course you are, but you're reckless, Angela, and I do feel . . .'

'Well?'

'You say you have "the sight". If so, isn't that all the more reason to shun people who—who dabble in occult things? I know so little about those—pursuits, but I'm sure they're dangerous.'

'Darling Demeter, of course they are, and would seem especially so to you.'

'I'm not particularly fond of that name—Demeter—not now.'

'But I believe Nichol was right about that, as about many things. You are her type, if not her incarnation. She was the mother of growth and beauty, and my "sight" tells me you will have splendid sons and daughters, a large family; that you'll be strong and beautiful to the end of your days, and that they and Geoffrey will be proud of you.'

'Oh Angela, I hope you're right.'

'I know I am.'

The two girls gazed at one another, and then Clare said: 'I never wanted you to use that gift of yours—for me, but if just this once you have "seen" for me, and it's true—why then, it's wonderful. And after all, it has nothing to do with Nichol. It was something which was born with you.'

'It's one of the few happy things I have seen for anyone,' Angela said. 'I believe he saw too, and knew he couldn't hurt you. What and who he was, I cannot say . . . not invulnerable, not possessed of absolute power, for I could deceive him, though I was in his power. He brought me here to make trouble for you all, you know.'

'But you didn't.'

149

'My heart wasn't in it. You have to wish people evil in your heart, before it can really affect them.'

'You won't ever wish that for anyone again, will you?' Clare entreated. 'You couldn't, for you've been really helped and rescued; given a fresh start.'

Angela said soberly, 'I'll try to make use of all the money I have. Not that I don't still want to have an exciting life but . . . since the one to help save me was poor old Phillis, I'd like to make a start with her. Would you trust me? She'd agree, I think, but I wouldn't like it to be an extra worry to you, if I took her.'

'You? Take her? What in the world do you mean?'

'I like her, poor old thing, and she's lonely. That's why she drank secretly, to forget she was lonely. She says she's cured of it, and I believe she is and won't relapse if she is happy and wanted. You've been awfully good to her, but it isn't possible for you to really *want* her. Becky bickers with her interminably, and she has nobody now Noel has gone.'

'He telephoned yesterday,' Clare said. 'He and Joan are married. Geoff thinks it may work out.'

'Probably it will. That girl is clever. He'll have to wear blinkers, but she'll look after him.'

'But do you seriously want to take poor Phillis away from here, to live with you?'

'Wouldn't it be a relief to you?'

'It makes me feel selfish and heartless, but yes, it would, if she could be happy elsewhere. Only – Angela – it seems so fantastic.'

'Why? I know what it means to be lonely. I'd be glad enough to have her in the background of my life, and she wouldn't be a burden to me. I shall buy a house in London, and engage somebody very kind and nice to look after her. I shan't always be with her, but I can always be in touch with her, and I can give her everything she wants. It would be a comfort to me, to have somebody dependent on me, who would grow to love me, and I think Phillis would. She's an affectionate soul. She'd have all the pretty things she wants, and treats, and the best doctors to keep her alive as long as possible.'

'It sounds like a fairy tale for her. But suppose you marry?'

'If I do, what difference will it make? Although her own marriage ventures were unfortunate, it would be a romance to her, and I'd look after her just the same, as though she were my grandmother.'

'It's for her to make the decision,' Clare said, stunned by the plan, but not denying its glittering possibilities.

'I shan't put the suggestion to her unless you approve.'

'But I do, of course, if you're sure. I've tried to do my best for them all. I would never have turned them out, but they've been a burden to me.'

'How could they be anything else? You and Geoffrey are starting life, and you've enough to do to cope with him.'

'And the housekeeping.' Clare laughed. 'I'm thankful Joan has gone, but yet I miss her terribly sometimes, and I've already made some frantic blunders.'

'Well, now you'll have Becky to contend with, and heaven knows she's no easy problem,' said Angela.

*

Becky, her nerves strained and her fortitude exhausted, was now determined to settle her own problem.

It was awful to have Marty going about her duties with a hard, stony face. Conversation was reduced to a minimum, for even Becky, who loved to talk, could not find pleasure in the sound of her own voice, when at the best she was answered only by monosyllables, and sometimes not answered at all.

Marty, she thought, must know as well as she knew that things could not go on like this for much longer. Obviously she was planning something or other. She wasn't a weak character to drift on indefinitely in this state of bottled-up resentment, and her grievance, whatever it was, must be voiced sooner or later.

Nevertheless, to contemplate a break with the one who had made her life possible for years, was enough to make even the stout-hearted Becky quail, and it was with an inward tremor, though with outward brusqueness, that she said one evening when Marty brought in her supper tray: 'I've no appetite. Who could have, when food is just slumped down before them in that take it or leave it way?'

Marty answered stonily, 'After next week you'll have to manage with Barbara or find someone else. I'm leaving.'

'I can't say I'm surprised to hear it, after the way you've behaved, but even you must own that I've the right to know why you're deserting me.'

'Yes, you've the right,' Marty agreed, 'if you don't already know, which it's more than likely you do.'

'Oh, sit down, woman, and talk like a human being,' Becky said impatiently. 'I've gone through enough lately, but you're so full of yourself that you're not considering that. It's all to do with that Robert Ellis, I suppose. The letter you had from America was from him.'

'Yes – it was. He wrote because he wanted to know how I was getting on.'

'He took his time. It must be the best part of ten years since he showed you a clean pair of heels.'

'And who was responsible for that?' Marty demanded in a trembling voice.

Becky welcomed this first sign of emotion, though deep within her she was frightened. She said, 'He was. He left you high and dry.'

'He wouldn't have done, but for you.'

'What nonsense! I don't know what you mean.'

'He says he's made good,' Marty said, her voice toneless again. 'He didn't have luck right away, in fact he was downright unlucky, but then he fell in with a man who had a shop in Brooklyn, who offered him a job – a bookshop it is; and they got on well together, and some months ago, this man took him into partnership, because he's growing old and wants to shift most of the work upon Bob. It's a thriving little business, Bob says, and he's asked me to go out there and marry him. He says in his letter that he'd have risked taking me with him when he first went to Canada, only he saw you, and you told him it would be downright unfair to me, with his poor prospects, and that you'd offered me employment which I'd accepted.'

'So it would have been unfair; he'd have dragged you into the gutter, and I *had* offered you employment, and glad enough you'd been to accept.'

'You never told me he'd called, that he'd seen you, that he'd said he was ready to marry me, but that you'd sent him off.'

'I thought it much better you shouldn't know.'

Marty cried out with passion, 'How dared you do such a thing? To take it on yourself, to treat me as a child, me who was a woman over thirty.'

'Now listen, Marty,' Becky said. 'You weren't in love with the man. He'd walked out on you and treated you vilely. He was a thorough bad hat. You knew it, you said it; you knew that, whatever happened, you would be much better off without him. If he really has made good, it's one of the seven wonders of the world. When he turned up at the theatre knowing you were my relief dresser, and it happened to be on a day when I didn't require you, I consented to see him, and one look at him was enough. I knew he'd never be any good to you; so I lied – yes, I admit I lied, but it was for a good purpose. I told him you wouldn't see him and had asked me to get rid of him, which I did; but if he'd been any sort of a man do you think he would have taken a dismissal from me? He'd have been determined to see you and nobody else, if he'd really wanted to marry you.'

'Did he say he wanted to marry me?' Marty asked in a low voice.

'Well, yes, he did – but if you had, he'd not have gone to Canada where it seems he may have pulled himself together. He'd have lived on your earnings to this day.'

'How could you?' Marty said brokenly. 'You knew I'd have married him because of the baby. I wouldn't have had to go through all that alone, disgraced and shamed.'

'You didn't go through it alone. I stood by you. You had your confinement very comfortably at my expense. Everyone was very sorry for you.'

'They wouldn't have had to be sorry for me, if he'd married me. My baby would have had a name, and she'd be with me, not adopted and gone from me; belonging to another woman, and me not even knowing where she is.'

'What good would it be for you to know? The only thing you could do was to make a clean break and a fresh start. Even if you *had* married, you'd have probably had to put her out to nurse with some poor family, because you'd have had to work to keep her. As it is, she was taken by well-to-do people and I've no doubt she's had every advantage.'

'Bob never knew I was expecting a baby. If you'd told him, it would all have been different.'

'Different and worse,' Becky said.

'You're a childless woman, and you don't know what it means to bring a child into the world and to have to part with her.'

'I'm not devoid of imagination,' Becky said drily. 'I know it was hard on you, but it would have been harder on the child if you hadn't. Have sense, Marty. What he says in his letter may not be true. If you went out to America to him, you'd very likely discover that for yourself. Do you think he's been without a woman in his life all these years? For all you know he may be married. He wrote to you on chance, I'd say, thinking that if you were still single you'd jump at him, and that you'd probably saved money, to put into his business, which you've only his word for it is prosperous.'

'You've no right to say such a thing, Miss Redcliffe. You don't know what sort of a man he is now.'

'Neither do you. You can't pretend that you've pined for him. You told me you never wanted to see him again. You were down and out, remember, when old Mrs Barry told me about you, said you'd had a nurse's training, and that you would be suitable to take over from her, from time to time. He'd had all your savings out of you, after he'd seduced you, and when you were down to rock-bottom, he deserted you.'

'He says in his letter he's ashamed to think of the way he treated me.'

'And well he might be, if he's got any shame in him. It'd take more than a sentimental letter to make any sensible woman believe in such a man, and to my mind it's a true saying that the leopard can't change his spots.'

'I don't care what you think about Bob. Perhaps it's true,

154

perhaps it isn't, but that doesn't excuse what you did to me. The deceit of it all these years, and me so grateful to you, willing to do anything for you, to give up my whole life because I never forgot the way you stood by me; paying out money for me, and taking me in after I left that Home. But now I can see how it was. It was as though you'd bought the rest of my life. You'd started to be ill, you knew you'd have to leave the stage, and that you'd have to have someone you could trust to look after you, someone who'd be faithful to you. It was yourself you were thinking of – not me.'

'That's grossly untrue,' Becky said indignantly. 'I couldn't force you to take the job with me and stay with me. You could have gone back to your nursing, but you preferred to be employed by me. I've paid you a good salary.'

'You'll be telling me next that I've not earned it.'

There was a quiet moment of silence before Becky replied, and then she said : 'No – I could never say that.'

'I've slaved for you,' Marty said. 'Three women couldn't have done for you all that I've done, and many a time I've sickened of it, and longed for the old hospital life. I've kept up with my old Matron, as you know, and she with her own private nursing home now. She'd be glad enough to have me there, but I wasn't to be tempted, though I've been buried here for the last years with no friends and no time to give to them, if I'd had any. It's been a cruel waste of all I can do, for not even you will deny that I'm a good nurse.'

'Of course I don't deny it.'

'But there's a limit to everything,' Marty went on, 'and I'm leaving. It could never be the same now between us.'

Becky said nothing. There was nothing more to say. Moreover, she was exhausted. She was too old for such scenes, she thought miserably, too old to care much what became of her. She would go into a nursing home, she supposed, for it would be far too much of an effort to find anyone who would be willing to live in this quiet place as her attendant. Besides, with Noel gone, and Phillis glorying in the fact that she would be living with Angela, life here wouldn't be the same. She had enjoyed lording it over them all; being the one with money who could dispense little treats, and gather them about her. Useless now to try to draw around herself the remnants of past glory. As an actress, she might be a legend, but as a human being, she was wanted by none.

'Your dinner will be cold. I'll heat it up for you,' Marty said, breaking the silence.

She bore away the covered dish to the kitchen, and Becky sat gazing drearily before her. Her little world, which had seemed so secure a week ago, had collapsed, and her courage had collapsed with it. Quentin had admired her and had thought her valiant, and she had meant to be valiant to the end, though there was no cure for her crippling disease and no cure for anno domini. She could have kept the flag flying, if Marty had stood by her, but now ... not now ...

Two tears trickled down her cheeks, to be followed by others. It was years since she had wept, and to the old and feeble, tears came as no relief – they were only a confession of failure.

Marty, returning after some delay with the reheated chicken casserole, came to a standstill as she surveyed Becky.

To her, the old woman, broken and weeping, was an awesome sight. Becky had had pain and trouble in plenty during the last few years, but never once had Marty seen her give way, not even when Quentin Moore had died, though for him she had truly grieved, and had, moreover, known that by his death her way of life was jeopardized.

Such pride, Marty had often thought with admiration and affection; such courage, though her once active and triumphant life had shrunk to the dimensions of a few rooms, a few people who still remembered that she was still alive, and the company of two old relations. Difficult she had often been, high-handed and arrogant, but she had never wept for herself, or for anyone else.

But now, because of me ... Marty thought, and was overwhelmed.

It might be that Becky cared little for her as a person, but as a nurse and companion she could not bear to part with her. It was something, thought Marty, sore of heart, and felt rising within her the old affection and pity which she had thought dead.

She put down the covered dish on the table, and said awkwardly: 'There now, tears won't help, and it's not as bad as all that, anyway.'

'It couldn't be worse,' Becky gulped. 'I've outlived my usefulness, my friends, my work, everything, and yet I can't die, though heaven knows I'd be glad to die.'

'Not you. You'll be feeling as spry as ever in the morning, and be wondering at yourself for giving way,' Marty said bracingly.

She put out a tentative hand to lay on Becky's shoulder, and found it seized and pressed feebly. 'I can't get on without you,' Becky confessed. 'I did wrong – I know it, but it wasn't all selfishness. I liked you, I wanted to help you, and I still say that man would have been of no use to you. Not even to keep the child would it have been worth marrying him. And children are a lottery. Many don't turn out well, and your baby was delicate, you know she was. Undivided attention and comfort and a country life was what she wanted, she couldn't have lived without it, and how could you have given her that, even if she had been born in wedlock?'

'I couldn't,' Marty said sadly, and with a deep sigh.

'But I should have told you what I had done. Many a time I've reproached myself for it, and been frightened that it might come out – as it has. I knew that if I did, you'd turn against me.'

'I haven't turned against you,' Marty said with an effort.

'You're leaving me.'

'Well, I thought I was, but . . .'

She released her hand from Becky's clutch, but only to put two consoling arms about the bent shoulders, and to draw the aged head against her comforting bosom. The very old were like children, Marty thought. They needed much the same treatment; to be loved and indulged, and occasionally scolded. They were even more helpless, poor souls, for children outgrew care and devotion, but the old needed it until the last hour of life.

'You mean you'll stay – after all?' Becky asked.

'Not here, I won't, and it wouldn't be good for you either, with the other two gone, especially if Mrs Deering has thoughts of selling the house, which a day or two ago she hinted to me she'd be glad to do. But I could look after you in London.'

'In London? Then you're not going to him – to New York?'

'I never really thought of doing that,' Marty confessed. 'There's so much water run under the bridge since I saw him, and it'd be a risk for any woman. But what I do want is another job, as well as this; a part-time job at nursing, which my old Matron has offered me more than once. I could still look after you, and train someone to attend to you when I wasn't there. Regent's Park is where I should be, and it may be you could get a house not too far away. You've talked sometimes of buying one, or you did after Mr Moore died.'

'Yes, I did. It's not a bad idea, Marty, for as you say, this place won't be the same without the other two, whatever Mrs Deering's future plans may be. I hated that flat, but a house would be different, and you – you'd share it with me. You wouldn't do night duty and leave me, would you?'

'Not me. I'd be only leaving you for a few hours each day, but it would be a change, and more real nursing. There's little enough you want of that. You'd pick up your friends again, if you were living within touch of them, and you'd not be depending on that Dr Irris, but could call in a really good specialist from time to time.'

'I'd like it,' Becky said, and allowed Marty to wipe her eyes, as she might have done had she been a child, 'though how I'll manage to move – at my age . . . let alone find a house.'

'Now you told me only a few weeks ago that Miss Beatrice Carr was trying to sell hers, and that's in St John's Wood, and you know the house and like it. If you were willing, I'd get you settled there in no time.'

Becky knew she was being managed, and perhaps for the first time in her life, she did not mind. She could trust Marty, who was incapable of tyranny. 'Well – I could write to Beatrice tomorrow,' she said.

'You do, and it'll mean a new lease of life for you – the

158

change and the shops and being more in the swim. But you're tired now, and here's your nice chicken, and when you've eaten some and had a glass of wine, you'll feel fine.'

Becky allowed herself to be coaxed to eat. She was steeped in a wonderful sense of peace, which was already shot through with an anticipation which renewed her vitality. She could have told Marty that she would lose little by her surrender; that when Becky died she would find she had been well rewarded financially, but she realized that, if this was said, there would never be the same relationship between them. Such calculations would never occur to Marty, and she might well feel she had been bribed, if Becky revealed to her that her future was secure.

But a different and more human reward was forthcoming before Becky slept that night, for as Marty settled her in bed, the old woman said : 'I'd want you to stay with me if you never again raised a finger for me. I'm fond of you, fonder than I've ever been of anyone. Just to have you around, means more to me than anything else in the world.'

*

By the time the spring came the theatre wing was empty and closed, and Clare knew that within months her first child would be born.

'So many changes in so short a time,' she said, as she and Geoffrey walked round the garden together one fine and blustery morning.

'Very satisfactory changes,' Geoffrey said.

'I suppose so. The old people were a tie and an anxiety, and they're all better off now, even Noel; but I miss them and I no longer care for this house.'

'We'll consider moving when the baby arrives,' Geoffrey said. 'Until then, you've promised me to take things quietly.'

'Oh, I will, though I've never felt better, and I'm gloriously happy, for you as well as for myself, Geoff darling.'

Certainly she bloomed in the promise of maternity, Geoffrey owned, for her face was radiant, her skin and hair both aglow with life, her eyes serene, her step buoyant. She had never been more beautiful, even though her body had thickened. He had been insane, he thought remorsefully, to have denied her this natural fulfilment for so long.

'Happy not only about the baby, but about your music,' Clare went on. 'When I hear the storm music played by a great orchestra, I shall be so proud, so glorified.'

'That won't be until the end of the year, and by then you'll have your hands full,' Geoffrey was amused. 'You'll probably expect me to compose cradle music.'

'Perhaps you will, just a tiny little thing for the baby. After all, other great musicians have composed lullabies.'

'Darling, I'm by no means a great musician.'

'You are. The storm music will make you great. You know what people think of it already.'

It was true that Geoffrey's publishers were excited about his latest composition, but it was too soon yet to be confident of its reception. The important thing was that he had at last created music which satisfied him, and which he believed would be the forerunner of even more satisfying work.

They stood hand in hand, and looked out upon the sea which was rough that morning, and Clare no longer hated it, or remembered its treachery. Least selfish of women, she yet was blissfully and unconsciously selfish in these months of burgeoning, for she had withdrawn into the small circle of her personal world. She was the guardian of a new life, and the death and destruction of the autumn were forgotten.